"Welcome Tory Marlowe."

She wanted to deny it, but his low voice, threaded with amusement, seemed to have taken away her ability to speak. Or maybe it was his sheer masculine presence, only inches from her.

Adam wasn't the boy he'd been at seventeen. That boy had haunted her dreams for a good long time. Grown-up Adam was twice as hard to ignore. He was taller, broader, stronger.

The lines around his eyes said he'd dealt with pain and come away cautious, but he had an air of assurance that compelled a response.

Books by Marta Perry

Love Inspired

A Father's Promise #41
Since You've Been Gone #75
*Desperately Seeking Daddy #91
*The Doctor Next Door #104
*Father Most Blessed #128
A Father's Place #153
Hunter's Bride #172
A Mother's Wish #185
A Time To Forgive #193

*Hometown Heroes

MARTA PERRY

wanted to be a writer from the moment she encountered Nancy Drew, at about age eight. She didn't see publication of her stories until many years later, when she began writing children's fiction for Sunday school papers while she was a church educational director. Although now retired from that position in order to write full-time, she continues playing an active part in her church and loves teaching a class of junior high Sunday school students.

Marta lives in rural Pennsylvania but winters on Hilton Head Island, South Carolina. She and her husband have three grown children and three grandchildren, and that area is the inspiration for the Caldwell clan stories. She loves hearing from readers and will be glad to send a signed bookplate on request. She can be reached c/o Steeple Hill Books, 300 East 42nd Street, New York, NY 10017, or visit her on the Web at www.martaperry.com.

A Time To Forgive
Marta Perry

Published by Steeple Hill Books™

STEEPLE HILL BOOKS

Steeple
Hill™

ISBN 0-373-87200-3

A TIME TO FORGIVE

Copyright © 2002 by Martha Johnson

This edition published by arrangement with Steeple Hill Books.

® and TM are trademarks of Steeple Hill Books, used under license.
Trademarks indicated with ® are registered in the United States Patent
and Trademark Office, the Canadian Trade Marks Office and in other
countries.

Visit us at www.steeplehill.com

Printed in U.S.A.

Speaking the truth in love,
we will in all things grow up into Him
who is the head, that is, Christ.
—*Ephesians* 4:15

Chapter One

Adam Caldwell stared, appalled, at the woman who'd just swung a sledgehammer at his carefully ordered life. "What did you say?"

The slight tightening of her lips indicated impatience. "Your mother-in-law hired me to create a memorial window for your late wife." Her gesture took in the quiet interior of the Caldwell Island church, its ancient stained-glass windows glowing in the slanting October sunlight, its rows of pews empty on a weekday afternoon. "Here."

He'd always prided himself on keeping his head in difficult situations. He certainly needed that poise now, when pain had such a grip on his throat that it was hard to speak. He put a hand on the warm, smooth wood of a pew back and turned to Pastor Wells, whose call had brought him rushing from the boatyard in the middle of a workday.

"Do you know anything about this?"

The pastor beamed, brushing a lock of untidy gray-ing hair from his forehead. "Only what Ms. Marlowe has been telling me. Isn't it wonderful, Adam? Mrs. Telforth has offered to fund not only the new window, but the repairs on all the existing windows. God has answered our prayers."

If God had answered Henry Wells's prayers in this respect, He'd certainly been ignoring Adam's. Adam glanced at the woman who stood beneath the largest of the church's windows, its jewel colors highlighting her pale face. She was watching him with a challenge in her dark eyes, as if she knew exactly how he felt about the idea of a memorial to Lila.

She couldn't. Nobody could know that.

He summed up his impressions of the woman—a tangle of dark brown curls falling to her shoulders, brown eyes under straight, determined brows, a square, stubborn chin. Her tan slacks, white shirt and navy blazer seemed designed to let her blend into any setting, but she still looked out of place on this South Carolina sea island. Slight, she nevertheless had the look of a person who'd walk over anything in her path. Right now, that anything was him.

"Well, now, Ms.—" He stopped, making it a question.

"Marlowe," she said. "Tory Marlowe."

"Yes." He glanced at the card she'd handed him. Marlowe Stained Glass Studio, Philadelphia. Not far from his mother-in-law's place in New Jersey. Maybe that was the connection between them. "Ms. Marlowe. Caldwell Island's a long way from home for you."

His South Carolina drawl was a deliberate contrast to the briskness she'd shown. A slow, courteous stone wall, that was what was called for here. "Seems kind of funny, you showing up out of the blue like this."

She lifted those level brows as if acknowledging an adversary, and he thought her long fingers tightened on the leather bag she carried. "Mrs. Telforth gave me a commission. I'm sorry Pastor Wells didn't realize I was coming. I thought Mrs. Telforth had notified him. And you."

"Also seems kind of funny that my mother-in-law didn't get in touch with me first."

Actually, it didn't, but he wasn't about to tell this stranger that. Mona Telforth blew in and out of his life, and his daughter's life, like a shower of palm leaves ripped by a storm—here unexpectedly, gone almost as quickly.

"I wouldn't know anything about that, but she spelled out her wishes quite clearly." The overhead fan moved the sultry air and ruffled the woman's hair. "She said she'd been thinking about this for some time, and she wants me to create a window that will be a tribute to her daughter's life and memory."

Pain clenched again, harder this time. Mona Telforth didn't know everything about her daughter's life. She never would. He'd protect her memories of Lila, but he wouldn't walk into this sanctuary every Sunday and look at a window memorializing a lie.

He inhaled the mingled scent of flowers and polished wood that always told him he was in the church. A place that meant peace to him had turned into a combat zone. "You have some proof of this, I suppose."

A soft murmur of dismay came from Henry. "I'm sure Ms. Marlowe is telling us the truth, Adam."

The woman didn't even glance toward the pastor. She was quick—he'd give her that. She'd already sized up the situation and realized he was the one she had to deal with, not Henry.

"I'm not a con artist, Mr. Caldwell. This commission is real. Take a look." She pulled an envelope from her oversize shoulder bag and thrust it toward Adam. If the paper had been heavier, she'd probably have thrown it.

The letter was definitely from Mona, written in the sprawling hand he recognized. And in spite of straying from the point a time or two, she made her wishes clear. She was aware of the deteriorating condition of the existing windows, and she'd fund all the repairs if she could have one window to honor her daughter's life. She'd even added the inscription she wanted on the window. *Lila Marie Caldwell, beloved daughter, wife, mother.*

If his jaw got any tighter, it would probably break.

Tory Marlowe seemed just as tense. Her hands clenched, pressing against her bag, as if she wanted to snatch the letter back. "Satisfied?"

"Ms. Marlowe, it's not a question of my being satisfied." He tried to identify the look in her velvet brown eyes when she wasn't actively glaring at him. It took a moment, but then he had it. Loneliness. Tory Marlowe had the loneliest eyes he'd ever seen.

A vague feeling of recognition moved in him. "Have we met before? You seem familiar to me."

She withdrew an inch or two. "No. About the commission—"

He tried to shake off the sense that he should know her. "My mother-in-law is a person of whims. I'm sure she was interested when she wrote this, but she's probably gone on to something else already." He could only hope. "You'd best go back to Philadelphia and look for another commission. This one isn't going to work out."

He saw the anger flare in her face, saw the effort she made to control it.

"It almost sounds as if you don't want a memorial to your late wife, Mr. Caldwell."

Now he was the one struggling—with grief, anger, betrayal. How could this woman, this stranger, cut right to the pain no one else even guessed at?

"Of course he does." Henry sounded scandalized.

The woman glanced at the pastor, startled, as if she'd forgotten he was there. Adam had almost forgotten Henry, too. He and Tory Marlowe had found their own private little arena in which to fight.

He shoved his emotions down, forcing them behind the friendly, smiling mask that was all his neighbors ever saw from him. "Pastor, you don't need to defend me. Ms. Marlowe is entitled to her opinion."

"But she didn't know Lila," Henry protested. "Why, Adam and Lila were the most devoted couple you could ever want to meet. Everyone loved Lila."

Everyone loved Lila. Including, Adam supposed,

the man she'd been running to when the accident took her life. For one insane moment he wondered what they'd say if he blurted the truth.

Speaking the truth in love, we grow up in all things into Christ... The Bible verse Grandmother Caldwell had given him on his baptism flitted through his mind, and he shook it off with a quick glance at the carved wooden baptismal font that stood near the pulpit. The truth couldn't be told about this. He might somehow, someday, be able to deal with Lila's desire to be rid of him. He couldn't ever forgive the fact that she'd been ready to desert their daughter.

Jenny. Determination hardened his will. Jenny idolized the mother she barely recalled, and she must never learn the truth. He had to keep his secret for her sake.

He rallied his defenses. "Both Ms. Marlowe and my mother-in-law are forgetting something, even if Mona does mean to go ahead with this."

Tory's long fingers closed around Mona's letter. "What's that?"

He managed a smile, knowing he was on firmer ground. "It's up to the church council to decide if they want a new window." He gestured toward the stained glass on either side of the sanctuary. "As you can see, we have a full complement of windows. I don't think they'll want to destroy one in order to build something different, no matter how generous the gift."

"They're going to lose one anyway, regardless of whether I replace it." She shot the words back. "Have you taken a good look at the second one on the left?"

"Such bad shape," Henry murmured. He walked to the window with the image of Moses and the burning bush. "It's one of the oldest ones. Is it really beyond hope?"

"It would probably shatter if we took it down for repair. I could rebuild it the way it is, but that wouldn't meet the terms of the commission." She moved to the window and outlined a fragment of rose glass, her finger moving as lovingly as if she touched a child. "It might be possible to save some of the pieces and incorporate them in the new window."

"Do you really think so?" Henry's eager tone sounded a warning note to Adam. Henry's enthusiasm would sweep the rest of the board along if Adam didn't find some way of diverting this project.

"You're being premature."

Henry and the woman swung around to face him, and for an instant they seemed allied against him.

Nonsense. This church was built and maintained by Caldwells, had been since the first Caldwell set foot on the island generations ago. Henry would side with him, not with a stranger.

"We can't do anything until I talk to my mother-in-law and find out if she really intends to pursue this project." Adam tried to smile, but his lips felt too stiff to move. "Frankly, I think you're here on a wild-goose chase, Ms. Marlowe. Naturally, if she has changed her mind, we'll cover your travel expenses back to Philadelphia."

Tory took a quick, impulsive step toward him, and again he had that sense of familiarity. Then she stopped, shaking her head. "That's very generous of you. But I don't think I'll be needing it."

"We'll see." He managed to smile and offer his hand. Hers was cool, long-fingered, with calluses that declared her occupation.

"Yes. We'll see."

He caught a trace of resentment in her tone as she dropped his hand and took a step away from him. She probably thought he was being unfair. Maybe so.

But the bottom line was that he had trouble enough living a necessary lie as it was. If he had to contend with this memorial—

He wouldn't. Which meant that Tory Marlowe, with her determined air and her lonely eyes, had to go back where she belonged.

He hadn't recognized her. Once both men were gone, Tory sank down in the nearest pew, hands clutching the smooth seat on either side of her. Adam Caldwell hadn't recognized her.

Well, of course not, some rational part of her commented. It was fifteen years ago, after all.

She'd seen a brief flicker of vague query in Adam's face when he'd looked at her. He'd asked if they'd met. Her response had been out of her mouth before she'd considered, but it had been the right one. If he didn't remember, she wouldn't remind him of that night.

It was silly for her to look back, sillier yet that Adam Caldwell sometimes drifted through her dreams like a Prince Charming she'd encountered once and lost.

She stared across the curving rows of empty pews, then focused on the window in front of her. In an example of stained-glass artistry that made her catch her breath, Jesus walked on the water of a glass sea, holding out His hand to a sinking Peter. Her gaze lingered on the gray-and-green glass waves.

Real waves had been slapping against the dock the night she'd pushed open the yacht club door—a fifteen-year-old visitor on her way to a dance, knowing nothing of the Caldwells for whom the island was named. One of her stepfather's golfing buddies had thrown out a casual invitation, probably because he'd wanted to make a favorable impression on a wealthy visitor.

She'd stood for a moment, watching couples move on the polished floor and be reflected in the wide windows that overlooked the water. The strains of music flowed over her, and her hands clenched nervously. She was an outsider, as usual.

Then someone tapped her lightly on the shoulder. She turned, heart thumping, to find a tall stranger holding out his hand.

"Dance?"

She looked into sea-green eyes in a boyishly handsome face. He smiled, and her heart turned over. Holding her breath, afraid to break the spell, she took his hand and followed him onto the dance floor. When his arms went around her, she felt as if she'd been waiting all her life for that moment.

They'd danced; they'd talked. They'd gone onto the

veranda and watched the moonlight on the water. Adam had plucked a white rose from a table arrangement and tucked it in her hair, calling her Cinderella, because she was the one unknown at the dance. It had been a fairy tale come true.

Right up until the moment she'd called to ask permission to stay later. She'd heard her mother weeping, her stepfather shouting. She'd raced out, hoping to get to them in time to avoid the inevitable. She hadn't.

She leaned back in the pew, staring dry-eyed at the window. That night had cut her past in two as cleanly as any knife, but she didn't cry about it any longer.

Probably she remembered Adam because she'd met him that particular night. She didn't believe in love at first sight or fairy-tale endings—they were for dreamy adolescents. Life had taught her that love, any kind of love, inevitably came with strings attached.

Adam didn't remember her, and that was for the best. If he had, it could only have led to an awkward conversation.

Of course, we danced together one night, didn't we? Whatever happened to you?

No, she certainly didn't want to have that conversation with an Adam Caldwell who was considerably more imposing than the seventeen-year-old he'd been then. Imposing, that was definitely the word. She glanced at the spot where he'd stood, frowning at her as if he didn't believe a word she was saying.

The friendly voice she remembered had deepened to an authoritative baritone, and Adam's hair had darkened to chestnut brown. He seemed broader, stronger. Life had given more wariness to his open face, added a few lines around his ocean-colored eyes.

But he still had that comfortable-in-his-own-skin air that said he was sure of himself and his place in the world. He was a Caldwell of Caldwell Island. And he still had that honeyed drawl that could send shivers down a woman's spine.

Maybe she'd better concentrate on the reasons she'd come back after all these years. With this commission, her fledgling stained-glass business was on its way. She'd never have to work for someone else or let another take credit for what she'd done.

For an instant her former fiancé intruded into her thoughts, and she pushed him away. Her engagement to her boss had confirmed a lesson she should have learned a long time ago—love always came with strings attached. Jason Lockwood had shown her clearly that he'd only love her if she did what he wanted.

Forget Jason. Forget everything except the reason you've come here. This memorial was her chance, and she wouldn't let it slip away because Adam Caldwell was, for some inexplicable reason, opposed to it.

More important, being here would let her fulfill the promise she'd made last year when her mother was dying. She'd finally erase the shadow Caldwell Island had cast over both their lives for too long. She wouldn't fail.

She focused on the image of Jesus' face in the window, the silence in the old church pressing on her.

Fredrick Bauer, her teacher, had always said a person couldn't work constantly in sanctuaries without being aware of the presence of God. Somehow she'd never been able to move past an adversarial relationship with the One Fredrick had insisted loved her.

Still, she knew God's hand was at work in bringing her here. Why else would she have found Mrs. Telforth's ad when she'd needed a reason to be here? Why else would her talents have been just what Mrs. Telforth needed?

You brought me here. If this is Your will, You'll have to give me a hand with Adam Caldwell. I don't know why, but I know he'll stop me if he can.

Tory was ready to take on Adam Caldwell again. She looked over the items she'd spread across the round oak table in the Dolphin Inn's small sitting room that evening. Her credentials, photos of windows she'd designed, the four-page spread in *Glass Today* magazine featuring a project she'd worked on.

Miranda Caldwell, who'd been working at the desk when Tory checked in, had insisted she use the sitting room for this meeting with Adam. The Caldwells who owned the island's only inn turned out to be Adam's aunt and uncle, making Miranda his cousin. The sweet-faced woman had been only too happy to talk about Adam.

He and Lila were so happy—her death devastated him.

Was that the reason for Adam's reluctance about the memorial window? Did he find his memories too painful? She paced restlessly across the room, stopping at the window to brush aside lace curtains and stare at boats rocking against a dock. Across the inland waterway, lights glowed on the mainland.

Adam's a real sweetheart, Miranda had said. Everyone's friend, the person the whole community relies on. And the family peacemaker, as well.

Tory didn't have much experience with family peacemakers. Her family could have used one. But she didn't think Adam intended to use his peacemaking skills on her.

A firm step sounded in the hallway. He was coming. She moved quickly to the table.

"Ms. Marlowe." Adam paused, filling the doorway.

She hadn't been as aware of his height and breadth in the high-ceilinged sanctuary. Here, there was just too much of him.

Her hands clenched. Concentrate on the work.

"I have some materials I thought you might be interested in." She gestured toward the table.

He didn't move. Instead he glanced around, as if it had been a while since he'd been in this room. His gaze went from sofa to mantelpiece to bookshelves. His eyes looked darker in the twilight, like the ocean on a cloudy day. He'd changed from the white shirt and khakis he'd worn earlier to jeans and a gray pullover that fit snugly across broad shoulders.

"My cousin Miranda must like you, if she's letting you use the family parlor."

"I didn't realize." She followed his gaze, suddenly off balance. Now that she looked around, it was obvious this was the family's quarters. She'd been too caught up in herself to notice. Photos of babies, children riding bicycles, fishermen holding up their catch, weddings—a whole family's history was written on these walls. Everything about the space was slightly faded, slightly shabby and obviously well loved. "I didn't mean to impose."

"Miranda wouldn't have told you to use the parlor unless she wanted you to." He crossed to the table, moving so quickly that she took an automatic step back and bumped into its edge. He reached out to flip through the photos she'd spread out. "You've had a busy afternoon."

Her efforts to impress him suddenly seemed too obvious. "I thought you might like to see projects I've worked on."

"Trying to convince me of your abilities?" His smile took the sting out of the words.

"Not exactly." She took a breath, trying to find the best way to say this. It was too bad diplomacy wasn't her strong suit. "This is an awkward situation. Your mother-in-law hired me, but it's important that you be satisfied with my work. After all, you knew your wife better than anyone."

The strong, tanned hand that flipped through the photos stopped abruptly. He pressed his fingers against the table until they whitened.

She'd made a mistake. She shouldn't have mentioned his wife, but how else could they discuss the memorial?

An apology lingered on her tongue, but that might

make things worse. She forced herself to meet his gaze. "I'm sorry if—"

He cut her off with an abrupt, chopping gesture. "Don't." He seemed to force a smile. "It's irrelevant, in any event. My mother-in-law chose you from all the people who answered her ad. She must have been satisfied with your ability to do what she wants."

"You've talked with her, then." She couldn't imagine that conversation.

"Yes." His lips tightened. "She's very enthusiastic about this project."

She might as well say what they both knew. "But you're not."

He shrugged. "Let's just say you caught me by surprise today and leave it at that. All right?"

There was more to it, but she wasn't in any position to argue. Not if the battle she'd anticipated was unnecessary.

"All right. I hope I can come up with a design that pleases both of you."

His gaze lingered on her face, as if he assessed her. She steeled herself not to look away from that steady gaze.

He frowned. "My mother-in-law has asked me to take care of all the details about this project."

"I see." She kept her voice noncommittal. "So you'll be supervising my work."

"I would in any event, since I'm chair of the church's buildings and grounds committee."

This wasn't any ordinary church business they were

talking about, but a memorial to his late wife. She had to show a little more tact.

"Perhaps you'd like to take with you some of my designs." She put the folder in his hand. "They might give you an idea of what would best memorialize your wife."

He dropped the folder, spilling photos onto the table. "No. Not now. Pastor Wells and I feel it best if you do the repair work first."

She stifled the argument that sprang to her lips. "Of course." She could only hope she sounded accommodating. "But I'll need to have some idea of what you want."

"Later." His tone didn't leave any room for argument. "We'll talk about it later."

The customer is always right, she reminded herself. Even when he's wrong.

"I'll start the analysis of the existing windows tomorrow then."

"I can be reached at the boatyard if you need me." He took a quick step away from the table, and she suspected only his innate courtesy kept him there at all.

"Mr. Caldwell, I..." What could she say? "I'm glad you've decided to go ahead with the project."

"It's my mother-in-law's project, not mine." Again she had the sense of strong emotion, forced down behind his pleasant, polite facade. "We'll both have to try and make her happy with it." He held out his hand, and she put hers into it. "Welcome to Caldwell Cove, Ms. Marlowe."

His firm grasp had as much ability to flutter her pulse now as when she'd been fifteen. Her smile faltered.

Don't be stupid, she lectured herself. The man means nothing to you. He never did.

Now if she could just convince herself of that, she might get through her second encounter with Adam Caldwell a little better than she had the first.

Chapter Two

At least Adam hadn't shown up yet with another reason she should leave the island and forget this project, Tory thought as she studied the church's east window the next morning. She half expected to hear his step behind her, but nothing broke the stillness.

She'd had an early breakfast at the inn, a place that seemed overly full of Caldwell cousins, all curious about her project. Then she'd hurried through the village of Caldwell Cove to the church, eager to begin but half-afraid she'd find another Caldwell waiting for her.

Adam had given in, she reminded herself. He'd agreed to his mother-in-law's proposal. So why did his attitude still bother her?

His face formed in her mind—easy smile, strong jaw, eyes filled with integrity. He had a face anyone would trust.

But Tory had seen the flash of feeling in his eyes

every time the memorial to his late wife was mentioned. She hadn't identified the emotion yet, but she knew it was somehow out of place.

Lila Caldwell had died four years ago. One would expect to see sorrow on her husband's face at the mention of her name. The feeling that darkened Adam's eyes was something much stronger than sadness.

Maybe the pastor and Miranda had it right. Perhaps Adam had loved his beautiful wife so dearly he still couldn't bear to discuss her. If so, that made her job more difficult.

The next time she saw him, she had to confront the subject. It was all very well to say she could begin with the repair work, but she should be working on the design for the new window. She had to get him to talk to her about it.

She moved up the stepladder to touch the intricate detail of the twined floral border around the window of Jesus and the children. Someone with pride in his craftsmanship and love for his subject had done that, choosing flowers to echo the children's faces instead of a more traditional symbol. A hundred years from now, she hoped someone might touch a window she'd created and think the same.

I can do this, can't I? She looked at the pictured face, longing for the love she saw there welling inside her. *Please, Lord, let me create something worthy of this place.*

If she did… How hard it was not to let self-interest creep in, even when she was planning something to God's glory. But she knew that success here could establish her business. For the first time since she was fifteen, she wouldn't have to scrape for every penny. She'd be able to pay her mother's final expenses and get a suitable stone to mark her grave. And she'd never have to rely on anyone else again.

The wooden outside door creaked. Tory's grip on the ladder tightened as she listened for Adam's confident tread. Instead, the patter of running feet broke the stillness. She turned.

The little girl scampering toward her had a tumble of light brown curls and a confident smile. A bright green cast on her wrist peeped out from the sleeve of a sunny yellow dress. She skidded to a stop perilously close to the ladder, and Tory jumped down.

"Hey, take it easy." She reached a steadying hand toward the child. "You don't want to add another cast to your collection, do you?"

The child smiled at her. Sunlight through stained glass crossed her face, and Tory saw that the cast matched her eyes. "I fell off the swing and broke my wrist," she said.

"You jumped off the swing." Adam's words quickly drew Tory's gaze to where he stood in the doorway. With the sun behind him, Tory couldn't see his expression, but she heard the smile in his voice. "And you're not going to do that again, are you, Jenny?"

This was his daughter, then, Tory's employer's granddaughter. *Jenny needs this memorial to her mother.* Mrs. Telforth's words echoed in her mind. *She does.*

The emphasis had seemed odd at the time. It still did.

Jenny sent her father an impish grin, then turned to Tory. "I got to be off school all morning to get my cast checked. Did you ever break anything?"

Adam reached the child and clasped her shoulders in a mock-ferocious grip. He was dressed a little more formally today than the night before, exchanging his khakis for dark trousers and a cream shirt. "Jenny, sugar, that's a personal question. You shouldn't ask Ms. Tory that when you don't even know her."

His daughter looked at him, brow wrinkling. "But, Daddy, that's how I'll *get* to know her."

Tory's lips twitched, as much at Adam's expression as the child's words. "I think she's got you there." She bent to hold out her hand to Adam's little girl. "Hi, I'm Tory. Yes, I broke my leg when I was nine. It wasn't much fun."

Jenny shook hands solemnly, her hand very small in Tory's. "But why not? Didn't you get a present for being a good girl when they put on the cast, and a chocolate cake for dessert, and an extra story?"

Tory's mind winced away from the memory of her stepfather berating her all the way to the emergency room for upsetting her mother while she lay in the back seat and bit her lip to keep from crying. "No, I'm afraid not. You're a lucky girl."

"She's a spoiled girl." But Adam didn't look as if the prospect bothered him very much. He smiled at his daughter with such love in his face that it hurt Tory's heart.

"I'm not spoiled, Daddy. Granny says I'm a caution." She frowned at the word, then looked at Tory. "Do you know what that means?"

"I suspect it means she loves you very much."

The frown disappeared. "Oh. That's okay, then."

"Jenny, love, let me get a word in edgewise, okay?"

Jenny nodded. "Okay, Daddy. I'll put water in the flowers. Don't worry, Granny showed me how." She scurried off.

"Sorry about that." Adam watched his daughter for a moment, then turned to Tory. "I really didn't come so Jenny could give you the third degree."

"She's delightful. How old is she?"

"Eight going on twenty, I think. I never know what she's going to come out with next."

His smile suggested he wanted it that way. Jenny didn't know how lucky she was. Tory realized she was seeing the Adam Miranda had described—the man everyone liked and relied on.

"That must keep life interesting." She wanted to prolong the moment. At least when they talked about his daughter they weren't at odds. They almost felt like friends.

"It does that." He glanced at the window. "Are you finding much damage?"

They were back to business, obviously. "Some of the windows are worse than others." She traced a crack in the molding around the image of Jesus and the children. "Settling has done this, but I can fix it."

Adam reached out to touch the crack. His hand

brushed hers, sending a jolt of awareness through her. He was so close, the sanctuary so quiet, that she could hear his breath. He went still for an instant, so briefly she might have imagined it.

"Let me know if you need any equipment. We might have it at the boatyard."

She nodded. She had to stop letting the man affect her.

"Look, Daddy. I brought the water." Jenny put a plastic pitcher carefully on the floor, spilling only a few drops, then skipped over to them. "You know what? I know what you're doing, Ms. Tory."

"Ms. Tory's fixing the windows for us, sugar."

She shook her head, curls bouncing. "Not just that. Everybody knows that. But I know she's gonna make a window for Mommy."

Tory happened to be watching his hand. It clenched so tightly his knuckles went white.

"Who told you that?"

"I did."

Tory blinked. She hadn't heard the church door open again, maybe because she'd been concentrating too much on Adam. A small, white-haired woman marched erectly toward them, a basket filled with bronze and yellow mums on her arm. The striped dress and straw hat she wore might have been equally at home in the 1940s.

"I told Jenny about the memorial window, Adam." She peered at him through gold-rimmed glasses. "Do you have a problem with that?"

"Of course not, Gran." Tory thought the smile he

gave his grandmother was a little forced, but he bent to kiss her cheek. "I was just surprised news traveled that fast."

"You ought to know how the island busybodies work by now." She turned to Tory, holding out her hand. "I'm Naomi Caldwell. You'd be the lady who's come to do the stained glass. Ms. Marlowe, is it?"

"Tory Marlowe. I'm pleased to meet you, Mrs. Caldwell."

The elderly woman must be in her seventies at least, if she was Adam's grandmother, but she had a firm grip and a bright, inquisitive gaze.

"I hear tell you're going to replace the Moses window."

"Does that bother you, Gran?" Adam sounded as if he hoped so.

His grandmother shook her head decidedly. "Never was up to the rest of the windows. If something's good, it'll improve with age."

Adam's expression softened. "Like you, for instance."

She swatted at him. "Don't you try to butter me up, young man."

She turned away, but Tory saw the glow of pleasure in her cheeks. For an instant she felt a wave of envy. If she'd had a grandmother like that, how different might her life have been?

"Jenny, child. Come help me with these flowers." Naomi Caldwell ushered Adam's daughter toward the pulpit, handing her the basket. "We'll put them on the dolphin shelf."

Tory tensed at the words. "The dolphin shelf?" She glanced at Adam, making it a question.

"That bracket behind the pulpit. A wooden carving of a dolphin once stood there. Gran likes to keep flowers in its place." Adam nodded toward the shelf where his grandmother was placing a vase.

I never meant for the dolphin to disappear. I didn't. Her mother's voice, broken with sobs, sounded in Tory's mind.

If she asked Adam about the dolphin, what would he say? Tory's mind worked busily. She had to find out more about the dolphin's disappearance if she were to fulfill her promise to her mother, but the last thing she needed was to stir up any additional conflict with Adam.

"What's this new window going to look like?" Mrs. Caldwell's question interrupted her thoughts before she could come up with an answer.

"That's really up to the family." Maybe she'd better stay focused on the window for the moment. "Usually I try to come up with some designs that reflect the person being honored, then let the family decide."

"How do you do that?" The woman paused, head tilted, her hands full of bronze mums. "Reflect somebody in a design, I mean." She seemed genuinely interested in the design, unlike everyone else Tory had met since she'd come to the island.

"Well, first I try to find out as much as I can about the person—her likes and dislikes, her personality, her background. Then—"

Carried away by the subject, she glanced at Adam.

His expression dried the words on her tongue. He stared at her, his eyes like pieces of jagged green glass.

"No." He ground out the word.

"What?" She blinked, not sure what he meant.

"I said no. You'll have to find another way of working this time."

Before she could respond he was calling the child, saying goodbye to his grandmother and walking out of the sanctuary.

The heavy door swung shut behind him, canceling the shaft of sunlight it had let in.

"I'm sorry about that." Adam's grandmother shook her head. "Reckon Adam's a bit sensitive about Lila."

"I see."

She'd made another misstep. She should have been more careful. But how on earth could she possibly find any common ground with Adam if he wouldn't even talk to her?

"I can't do this." Adam had arrived at his office at Caldwell Boatyard after dropping Jenny at school, his stomach still roiling. He'd found his brother, Matthew, waiting for him.

"Can't do what?" Matt perched on the edge of Adam's cluttered desk, toying with the bronze dolphin paperweight Lila had given Adam in happier times. Matt looked as if he had all the time in the world.

"Help that woman design a memorial window for Lila, of all things." Adam slumped into the leather chair behind the desk. Matt was the only person in the world he'd speak to so freely, because Matt was the only one he'd told the whole story to. A good thing he had his brother, or he might resort to punching the paneling. "If my mother-in-law wanted a window, why didn't she put it in her own church instead of saddling me with it?"

"Maybe because St. Andrews was Lila's church," Matt offered helpfully.

Adam glared at him. "Don't you have work to do? Or doesn't running a weekly paper and being husband and stepfather for two whole months keep you busy enough?"

"Actually, I am working." Matt smiled, his face more relaxed than Adam had seen it in years. Marriage seemed to agree with him. "Sarah and I want to do a story for the *Gazette* about the church windows."

"Great. That's just what I need." Adam rotated his chair so he could stare at the sloop he was refitting for an off-island summer sailor. "Maybe you can satisfy Tory Marlowe's curiosity."

He glanced at his brother, wondering how much he wanted to say about Tory. Everything, probably.

Matt lifted an eyebrow. "Curiosity?"

"She wants to talk about Lila." His throat tightened. "She wants to get to know her so she can create a fitting memorial."

Matt whistled softly, obviously understanding all the things Adam didn't say out loud. "What are you doing about it?"

"Not telling her the truth, that's for sure." He rubbed his forehead as if he could rub the memories away. He and Lila had married too quickly, too young, and he faulted himself for that as much as Lila. He hadn't realized until later, carried away as he was, that Lila had had totally skewed ideas of what their married life would be like. She'd hated the island, and everything he'd done to try and make things better only seemed to backfire. Even their beautiful baby hadn't made Lila want a real family.

She'd craved excitement, and eventually she'd found that with a man she'd met on one of her frequent trips to visit friends who, she claimed, were living the life she should have had.

He frowned at Matt. "I certainly can't tell her the truth. I'm not telling her anything, if I can help it."

"Sounds like a mistake to me."

"Why?" He shot the word at his brother like a dare, but Matt looked unaffected.

"You'll just encourage her to go to other people for what she needs."

"No one knows the truth."

Matt shrugged. "You're probably right. But what if you're not? Better answer her questions yourself than have her asking around town."

Unfortunately, that sounded like good advice. He lifted an eyebrow at Matt.

"How did you get to know so much about women, little brother?"

Matt grinned. "My wife's training me." He sobered. "Seriously, Adam. Just get through it the best you can. Give the woman a few noncommittal details and say you trust her artistic sense to come up with the design. She'll get busy with the design and stop bothering you."

"I hope so." But somehow he didn't think Tory was the kind of person to do anything without doing it to perfection.

He got up slowly, letting the chair roll against shelves crammed with shipbuilding lore. "Guess I'd better go back to the church and make peace with her, if I can."

Adam slipped in the side door to the sanctuary and stopped in the shadows. Tory, on the ladder, didn't seem to hear him. He could take a minute to think what he'd say to her.

Unfortunately he wasn't thinking about that. Instead he was watching her, trying to figure out what it was about the woman that made it so hard to pull his gaze away.

She wasn't beautiful. That was his first impression. At least, she wasn't beautiful like Lila had been, all sleek perfection. But Tory had something, some quality that made a man look, then look again.

Those must be her working clothes—well-worn jeans, sneakers, a T-shirt topped by an oversize man's white shirt that served to emphasize her slender figure. She looked like what she was, he supposed. An artisan, a woman who worked with her hands and didn't have time or inclination for the expensive frills that had been so important to Lila.

Tory's hair, rich as dark chocolate, had been pulled back and tied at the nape of her neck with a red scarf.

The hair seemed to have a mind of its own, as tendrils escaped to curl against her neck and around the pale oval of her face.

Oh, no. He'd been that route before, hadn't he? Intrigued by a woman, mistaking a lovely face for a lovely soul, thinking her promises meant loyalty that would last a lifetime. With Lila, that lifetime had only lasted five years before she'd lost interest in keeping her vows.

His hands clenched. He wouldn't do that again. He had his daughter, his family, his business to take care of. That was enough for any sensible man.

The smartest thing would be to avoid Ms. Tory Marlowe entirely, but he couldn't do that. Thanks to Mona's bright idea, he and Tory were tied inextricably together until this project was finished.

Something winced inside him. He had to talk to her, and it might as well be now.

He took a step forward, frowning. Tory had leaned over perilously far, long fingers outstretched to touch some flaw she must see in the window.

"Hold it."

She jerked around at the sound of his voice, the ladder wobbling. His breath caught as she put a steadying hand on the wall. He hurried to brace the ladder for her, annoyed with himself for startling her.

She frowned at him. "Are you trying to make me fall?"

"Sorry. I didn't mean to startle you. I'm trying to keep you from falling." He gave the elderly wooden ladder a shake. "This thing isn't safe."

She jumped down, landing close enough for him to smell the fresh scent that clung to her. "I do this all the time, you know. Scrambling around on rickety ladders comes with the territory."

"You might do that elsewhere, sugar, but not in my church."

Her dark eyes met his, startled and a little wary. The red T-shirt she wore under the white shirt seemed to make them even darker. "What did you call me?"

"Sorry." But somehow he wasn't. "Afraid that slipped out. It's usually Jenny I'm lecturing about dangerous pastimes."

Her already firm jaw tightened. "I'm not eight, and I'm doing my job."

She reminded him of Gran, intent on doing what she wanted to no matter how well-intentioned her family's interference was. The comparison made him smile.

"Are you always this stubborn?"

"Always." Something that might have been amusement touched her face. "I'm not your responsibility."

"Well, you know, there's where you're wrong. In a way, you are my responsibility."

She lifted level brows. "How do you figure that?"

He patted the ladder, and it shook. "Everything about the building and grounds of St. Andrews is my responsibility. Including rickety ladders."

She grimaced. "I've been on worse than this one, believe me."

"You shouldn't be up on a ladder at all." An idea

sprang into his mind, and it was such a perfect solution he didn't know why it hadn't occurred to him sooner.

Steel glinted in Tory's eyes. "If you think I'll give up the project because I have to climb a ladder, you have the wrong impression of me, Mr. Caldwell."

"Adam," he corrected. "I think my impression of you is fairly accurate, as a matter of fact. But I was referring to the ladder, not your personality, Ms. Marlowe."

A faint flush stained her cheeks, and she fingered the fine silver chain that circled her neck. "Maybe you'd better make that Tory. What about the ladder?"

"It's not safe. I'll have a crew come over from the boatyard to put up scaffolding so you can inspect the windows safely. That's what we should have done to begin with."

He was taking charge of the situation. That, too, was what he should have done from the word *go,* instead of letting himself get defensive.

"You don't need to—"

"As far as working on them is concerned—" he swept on "—we'll take the panels out completely. That way we won't have to worry about St. Andrews getting slapped with a lawsuit."

He thought her lips twitched. "Is that what you're worried about?"

"Definitely."

She nodded. "Well, in that case, since you're being so cooperative, I will need a workroom, preferably with good light, where things won't be disturbed."

She glanced around. "Is there a space in the church that would do?"

"Nothing," he replied promptly. Ms. Tory didn't know it, but she was walking right into his plans. "We have just what you need at the house, though. It's a big room with plenty of light and a door you can lock. We'll move in tables or benches, whatever you need."

He could see the wariness in her face at the idea. "I don't think I should be imposing on you."

"It's not an imposition. It's my responsibility, remember?"

"Having me work at your home sounds well beyond the call of duty. I'll be in your way."

"You haven't seen our house if you think that. It's a great rambling barn."

"Even so…" She still looked reluctant.

"You don't want me to bring up the big guns, do you?"

"Big guns?"

"Pastor Wells and my grandmother. They'll agree this is the best solution. You'd find them a formidable pair in an argument."

The smile he hadn't seen before lit her face like sunlight sparkling on the sound. "Thanks, but I think you're formidable enough. All right. We'll try it your way."

"Good." He was irrationally pleased that she'd given in without more of a fight. "I'll have a crew over here later this afternoon to set up scaffolding, so you can inspect the rest of the windows tomorrow. Don't climb any ladders in the meantime."

She lifted her brows at what undoubtedly sounded like an order. "Are you always this determined to look after people?"

"Always."

She turned to grasp the ladder. He helped her lower it to the floor. Her hair brushed his cheek lightly as they moved together, and he had to dismiss the idea of prolonging the moment.

Just get through it, Matt had said. Okay, that's what he'd do. He'd take control of this project instead of reacting to it. And the first step in that direction was to have Tory's workroom right under his eyes. Of course that meant that Tory herself would be, as well.

He could manage this. All right, he found her attractive. That didn't mean he'd act on that attraction, not even in his imagination.

Chapter Three

"Well, what do you think? Will this be a comfortable place to work?"

Adam looked at her for approval. Light poured into the large room he called the studio from its banks of windows. On one side Tory could see the salt marsh, beyond it the sparkle of open water. At the back, the windows overlooked a stretch of lawn, then garden and stables. Pale wooden molding surrounded the windows, and low shelves reached from the sills to the wide-planked floor. Anyone would say it was an ideal place to work.

"This should do very nicely." She couldn't say that his home had taken her by surprise. This wasn't a house—it was a mansion. And she didn't want to say that she'd lived like this once, before her mother's downward spiral into depression, alcoholism and poverty.

She took a breath. She'd been handling those recollections for a long time. She could handle this reminder. Besides, being here was a golden opportunity to find out what she needed to about the Caldwells. She just had to get Adam to open up.

"Why do you call it a studio?"

He shrugged. "We always have. My mother used it that way. Dad turned the space into a playroom for us kids after she died." He pointed to a small easel in the corner, the shelves behind it stacked with children's books, paints and crayons. "Jenny likes to paint in here when she's in the mood."

The room seemed uncomfortably full of his family with one notable exception. He hadn't mentioned his wife. "Was your mother an artist?"

"She painted, did needlework, that kind of thing." Sadness shadowed Adam's face for a moment. "I can remember her sitting in front of the windows with some project on her lap. She died when I was eight."

"I'm sorry." Tory had been five when her father died. She hesitated, torn. If she told Adam about it, that might create a bond that would encourage him to talk, but she didn't give away pieces of herself that easily.

She walked to the long table that held the first of the panels they'd removed from the church that morning. Everything she'd asked for was here, ready and waiting for her. She longed to dive into the work and forget everything else. If Adam would leave—

"What about you?" Adam leaned his hip against the table, crossing his arms, clearly not intending to go anywhere at the moment.

She looked at him blankly, not sure what he meant by the question.

"Family," he added. "You've met Jenny and my grandmother, heard about my mother. What about your family?"

It was the inevitable question Southerners put to each other at some point. She'd heard it before, phrased a little differently each time, maybe, but always asking the same thing. Who are your people? That was more important than what you did or where you went to school or even how much money you had. Who are your people?

"I'm alone." That wouldn't be enough. She had to say more or he'd wonder. "My father died when I was quite young, and my mother last year. I don't have any other relatives." At least, not any relatives that would like to claim me.

"I'm sorry." Adam's eyes darkened with quick sympathy. "That's rough. They were from this part of the world, weren't they?"

The question struck her like a blow. "What makes you think that?"

He smiled slowly. Devastatingly. "Sugar, you've been slipping back into a low-country accent since the day you arrived. You can't fool an old geechee like me."

Geechee. She hadn't heard that word since she'd left Savannah, but it resounded in her heart. Anyone born along this part of the coast was a geechee, said either affectionately or with derision, depending on the speaker. Apparently she couldn't leave her heritage behind, no matter how she tried.

Tory managed a stiff smile in return. "I'm from Savannah originally, but I've been up north so long I thought I passed for one of them."

"Not a chance." He pushed himself away from the table, the movement bringing him close enough to make her catch her breath, making her too aware of the solid strength of him. "Welcome back home, Tory Marlowe."

She wanted to deny it, to say she didn't have any intention of belonging in this part of the world again. But his low voice, threaded with amusement, seemed to have taken away her ability to speak. Or maybe it was his sheer masculine presence, only inches from her.

Adam wasn't the boy he'd been at seventeen. That boy had been charming enough to haunt her dreams for a good long time. Grown-up Adam was twice as hard to ignore. He was taller, broader, stronger. The lines around his eyes said he'd dealt with pain and come away cautious, but he had an air of assurance that compelled a response.

A response she didn't have any intention of making. She wouldn't let fragments of memory turn her to mush. She'd better get back to business, right now.

She cleared her throat, dismissing its tightness. "One thing about working in the studio concerns me."

He lifted an eyebrow. "Only one?"

She would not return that attractive smile. "Glass

slivers fly around when I'm working. And the lead I use is dangerous to children.''

He nodded, face sobering. ''I've told Jenny she must never come in unless you invite her. To be extra safe, I have a key to the studio for you.'' Adam held out a key ring. ''And a house key, in case you ever need to come in when no one is here.''

It was as if he handed her a key to the Caldwell family. Everything she was hiding from him flooded her mind. ''I won't need that.''

He took her hand and put the ring in her palm, his fingers warm against hers. ''Just in case.'' We trust you, he seemed to be saying.

You can't. You can't trust me.

''Looks as if you're getting all set up in here.'' A tall, silver-haired man paused in the doorway, his interruption saving her from blurting something that would defeat her goals even before she started.

Adam took his hand away from hers, unhurried. ''Tory, this is my father, Jefferson Caldwell.''

''Mr. Caldwell.'' He came toward her, and she shook his hand while she tried to ignore the voice in her mind.

Jefferson and Clayton Caldwell. Her mother's words had been disjointed and hard to follow. *They were brothers, just a year apart.* Her mother's co-quettish giggle had sounded out of place in the hospital room. *They were both sweet on me, you know.*

Tory could easily imagine that. She'd seen pictures of her mother at fifteen, before alcohol and sorrow had weighed her down. Emily had been a golden girl, far more beautiful than Tory could ever dream of being.

If she mentioned Emily Brandeis's name to Jefferson Caldwell, would he remember that long-ago summer? Her mother had certainly remembered it. Rational or not, she'd traced everything that had gone wrong in her life to the events of that summer.

Jefferson surveyed the setup that had changed his studio into her workroom, then turned to her. "Welcome to Caldwell Island, Ms. Marlowe. I hope you're finding everything you need for this project."

Jefferson's beautifully tailored jacket and silky dress shirt gave him an urbane, sophisticated air that seemed out of tune with the down-home impression she received from his brother, Clayton, whose family ran the inn.

"Yes, thank you. I hope it won't inconvenience you to have my workshop here."

"Not at all." He waved his hand as if to encompass the entire estate. "Twin Oaks is a big enough place to accommodate all of us."

"It's a beautiful house." She said what he no doubt expected.

"Yes, it is that." Jefferson smiled with satisfaction at her words.

A cold house, she thought, but who was she to judge? No house could be more frigid than her grandmother's mansion in Savannah.

The hospital where she'd sat beside her mother's bed hadn't been far from her grandmother's Bull Street mansion, but there'd been no contact. Neither of them had expected it. Amanda Marlowe had long since cut all ties with her embarrassing daughter-in-law. Probably losing touch with her granddaughter had seemed a small price to pay.

Her mother had moved restlessly on the bed, shaking her head from side to side. *I didn't mean for him to take his family's heirloom. I didn't mean it, Tory. I didn't want anyone to get hurt.* Tears had overflowed. *You have to find the dolphin and put it back. Promise me.* Her thin hand had gripped Tory's painfully. *Promise me. You have to promise me.*

I didn't mean for him to take it. Her mother had felt responsible for the disappearance of the carved dolphin from the island church. For reasons Tory would never understand, that guilt had haunted her during her final illness. Someone had been hurt, but who?

I didn't mean for him to take it. One of the Caldwells, obviously, but which brother? Jefferson or Clayton?

She searched for something to say to drown out her mother's voice in her mind. "I'm staying at the Dolphin Inn, you know. So I've become acquainted with your brother and his family."

Jefferson's face froze as a chill seemed to permeate the air. "I suppose they're making you as comfortable as they can. When the new Dalton Hotel is finished, we'll be able to offer visitors something better than Clayton's little operation."

The spurt of malice in his words silenced her. Had he really just insulted his brother to a stranger?

Luckily Jefferson didn't seem to expect a response.

"I'll let you get on with your work. Please ask if there's anything else you need." He turned and left the room before she could find a response.

When Jefferson's footsteps had faded down the hallway, she gave Adam a cautious look. "Did I say something I shouldn't?"

He shrugged, but she could almost feel the tension in his shoulders. "Nothing you could have known about, so don't worry. My father and his brother have been on the outs for a long time. The rest of us have learned to take it for granted."

The silence stretched between them, broken only by a bird's song drifting through the open window. How long a time, she wanted to ask. Since they were teenagers? Since Emily Brandeis came to the island and the dolphin vanished from the church?

But she couldn't ask because she wasn't ready for these people to know who she was yet. Until she knew how they'd respond, she couldn't risk it.

"I'm sorry for putting my foot in it," she said carefully. "Family feuds can be devastating." Nobody knew that better than she did.

"I'm used to it."

Was he? Or was that merely a convenient thing to believe?

One thing was certain. Her job on the island wasn't just another commission or a step toward the independence she longed for or even a chance to keep her promise.

Like it or not, her history and Adam's history were interwoven in ways he couldn't begin to imagine.

* * *

What was she thinking? Adam leaned against the heavy oak table, watching Tory's face. Light from the bank of windows made her hair glint like a raven's wing.

He forgot, sometimes, how odd the Caldwell family feud must seem to an outsider, especially since he had no intention of telling this particular outsider anything else. She didn't need to know that his father's drive for success at any cost had created a wedge between him and the rest of the family, who thought he'd left his honor behind along the way.

She also didn't need to learn that Adam's peacemaker role had grown increasingly difficult over the years. He'd been peacemaker between his father and brother, between his father and the rest of the family—maybe the truth was that the buffer always ended up battered by all sides.

"It must bother you." Her eyes went soft as brown velvet with sympathy.

That look of hers would be enough to melt his heart if he didn't watch out. "I suppose it does, sometimes." She was a stranger, he reminded himself. Furthermore, she was a stranger whose presence here threatened his secret.

Get through it, his brother had said. Matt charged at problems headlong, shoving barriers out of his way. Adam wasn't Matt.

He'd come up with another way of dealing with the trouble represented by Tory Marlowe. His gaze was drawn irresistibly to her. What was she thinking?

Apparently assuming he wasn't going to say anything else, she bent over the window panel, her fingers tracing the pieces as lovingly as he'd touch his daughter's hair. Her dark locks were escaping from the scarf that tied them back. They curled against her neck as if they had a mind of their own.

Deal with her, he reminded himself. Not gawk at her as if you've never seen a woman before.

He didn't want her wandering around Caldwell Cove, digging into a past that was best forgotten. So the best solution, until and unless he could find a way to derail this memorial window altogether, was to move Tory into Twin Oaks.

"I've been having second thoughts about this arrangement."

She looked up, startled. Apparently while he was watching the way her hair curled against her skin, she'd forgotten he was in the room. "What do you mean? I thought you wanted me to work here."

Would he ever get things right with this woman? He reminded himself that it didn't matter—all that did was her leaving Caldwell Cove.

"Of course I want you to work here." He almost put his hand on her shoulder, then decided that would be a bad idea. "In fact, I think you ought to stay here at the house while you're in Caldwell Cove."

A frown line appeared between her brows. "Is this because of the feud between your father and his brother?"

He should have realized she'd think that. "Absolutely not," he said. "I get along fine with Uncle Clayton and everyone else in the family."

"Well, you would." Her lips curved in the slightest of smiles. "Miranda says you're everyone's friend. That everyone in town relies on you."

"I wonder if she meant that as a compliment." That was him, all right. Good old reliable Adam.

"Of course she did. Anyone would."

"Sounds sort of stodgy, don't you think?"

"It sounds good." She looked startled, as if she hadn't intended to say that. "Anyway, if it's not that, then why should I move here from the inn? I'm comfortable there, and I can drive over every day."

Because I want to keep tabs on you. He could give her any reason but the real one.

"We have plenty of room for you."

"They have room for me where I am."

"Yes, but you won't have to pay for a room here."

She blinked at that, face suddenly shadowed. The look opened up a whole new train of thought. Was money a problem?

"I don't know what advance my mother-in-law has paid you," he said cautiously. Tory obviously had an independent streak a mile wide. "But it stands to reason we should pick up your expenses while you're here."

"That doesn't mean I should be your houseguest."

"It doesn't mean you shouldn't." He suspected he sounded the way he did when he tried to coax Jenny into eating her collard greens. "If you move into Twin

Oaks, you'll be close to your work. That will certainly be more convenient.''

Her lips pursed as she considered, and he found himself wondering how it would feel to kiss those lips. He shook off the speculation. Not a good idea, Caldwell.

''If you're worried about propriety, you needn't be. As my father said, it's a big house. Miz Becky, the housekeeper, lives in, and we often have business colleagues of my father's staying.''

''That isn't what I'm worried about.'' She looked up, eyes dark and serious. ''I might even find it helpful—giving me a better sense of the kind of person your late wife was.''

It felt as if she'd punched him, and he could only hope his expression didn't change. Naturally she'd think living in Lila's house, talking with the people who'd been closest to her, would help her know Lila.

Nobody here will tell you the truth, Tory, because nobody knows it but me.

Well, Miz Becky might have guessed some of it. The Gullah woman who'd taken care of the family since his mother died often knew things no one had told her. But Miz Becky would never betray his trust, no matter what Tory asked. She understood loyalty.

He managed a smile. ''What's holding you back?''

''Your father.''

''Dad?'' That startled him. ''Why on earth?''

''I didn't get off to a good start with him. I can't imagine that he'd want me living under his roof.''

"Now that's where you're wrong. He's the one who suggested it."

Get her out of Clayton's place, for pity's sake, his father had said irritably. That's the last impression we want to make on the woman—that Caldwells are back-country hicks with no more ambition than to rent out a few rooms and go fishing.

"Is that true?"

"Cross my heart," he said lightly. "Dad would like you to stay here."

"And you would like me to leave the island and never come back." Her eyes met his.

She wouldn't be convinced by a polite evasion. His natural instinct was to say as little about Lila as possible. As long as he didn't talk about her, he could forget. At least, that's what he told himself.

Tory's gaze was unwavering. He felt a surge of annoyance. No one else in his life pushed him on this. They respected his grief and kept silent.

Or maybe that was the pattern of his relationships. He was the listener, the shoulder to cry on. He wasn't supposed to have tears of his own.

"All right." He blew out a frustrated breath. "I'm not crazy about this idea of Mona's."

"That's been clear all along. But I don't understand why. A memorial to your wife…"

"Exactly. A memorial. Something that brings back memories." He swung away from her, not wanting her to discover what kind of memories they were.

"I'm sorry." Her voice softened, filled with sympathy for the grief she imagined he was expressing.

"I don't want to hurt you, and I'm sure that's the last thing on your mother-in-law's mind."

"Thank you." She shamed him with her quick sympathy. For an instant he imagined the relief he'd feel at telling her the truth.

Horrified, he rejected the thought. He couldn't tell anyone, least of all a stranger working for Lila's mother. Mona, like Jenny, would never know the truth from him. He turned toward her.

"Look, this will work out. Just give me time to get used to the idea. All right?"

Tory nodded. Her dark eyes shimmered with unshed tears, and he felt like a dog for accepting the sympathy he didn't deserve.

"All right. And if you're sure about this, I'll take you up on your offer of a room."

Relief swept through him. "I'm sure."

Tory squeezed his hand, the gesture probably intended to express sympathy. He felt the touch of her fingers right up his arm.

His eyes met hers. Her dark eyes widened, and her lips formed a silent *oh*. She felt what he did. And she didn't know what to do with it, either.

This is a mistake. The voice inside his head was deafening. You won't risk feeling anything for a woman again. And if you wanted to, it wouldn't be Tory. She's complicating your life enough just by being here.

Good advice. That was his specialty, giving good advice to other people. Why did he feel that following his own advice was going to be next to impossible where Tory Marlowe was concerned?

If she'd thought living at Twin Oaks would bring her any closer to her goals, Tory had been wrong. She hadn't found out a single thing about Lila or the disappearance of the dolphin in the three days she'd been there.

She leaned against the back porch post, sketch pad on her lap. The lawn, greening again after summer's heat, stretched under live oaks draped with Spanish moss that looked like swags of gray-green lace. Bronze and yellow chrysanthemums spilled over the flower beds along the walks.

Jenny lazed away a Saturday afternoon, pushing herself back and forth in a wooden plank swing suspended from a sturdy branch. Her sneakers scraped the ground with each arc, and her curls bounced.

Tory looked from the child to the sketch that had grown under her fingers. Jenny swung on the page, face lifted to the breeze she was creating.

"That's good, that is."

Tory glanced up. Miz Becky, the woman who ran Twin Oaks and apparently everyone in it, settled in the bentwood rocker.

"Thanks." Tory flexed her fingers and stretched, lifting damp hair off her neck. Even in fall, the air was sultry here. "I can't sit without doodling."

Miz Becky's smile warmed her elegant, austere face. With her hair covered by a colorful scarf wound into a turban, she looked like royalty. "Know what you mean about that.'' She lifted the strainer of fresh green beans. ''I got to keep my hands busy, too.''

It was the first time she'd been alone with Miz Becky, her first opportunity to ask her about Lila Caldwell if she wanted.

''How're those windows at the church coming along?'' Miz Becky asked.

''Not bad.'' Tory wrapped her arms around her knees, wishing she could find a tactful way to broach the subject. ''The repairs are moving along. Unfortunately, the new window isn't.''

The woman popped the ends off the beans with a decisive snap. ''Why's that?''

''I really need to find out more about Mrs. Caldwell's life if I'm going to come up with a design to honor her. So far—''

''So far Adam's not talking.'' Mix Becky tossed a handful of beans into a sweetgrass basket.

''That's about the size of it.'' She thought of the darkness that crossed Adam's open, friendly face whenever the topic was raised. ''I don't want to intrude on his grief, but I'm afraid I'll have to.''

''Grief?'' Miz Becky seemed to consider the word. ''I'm not so sure that's what's keeping him close-mouthed about her.''

Tory glanced up, startled. That almost sounded as if…

Before she could respond, Jenny ran toward them.

''Miz Tory, could we go for a walk on the beach?'' The child hopped onto the first step and balanced on

one foot. "Please?" She gave Tory the smile that was
so like her father's. "I can't go by myself."

She couldn't resist that smile. "If Miz Becky says
it's okay."

"Get along." Miz Becky flapped a hand at them.
She held Tory's gaze for an instant. "Just might answer a few questions for you."

Was the woman suggesting that Jenny could be a
source of information? Adam would definitely disap-
prove of that.

Jenny grasped Tory's hand and tugged her off the
step. "Come on. I'll race you."

Grabbing the sketch pad, Tory followed. She
wouldn't ask the child. If Jenny volunteered anything,
that was different.

They crossed the lawn. Jenny skipped ahead of her
down the path toward the beach. Palmettos and pines
lined it, casting dense shadows littered with oversize
pinecones and palmetto fans stripped by the wind.

They emerged from tree shadows into bright, clear
light, the ocean stretching blue, then gray, then blend-
ing into the sky at the horizon. Tory tilted her head
back, inhaling the tang of salt and fish and seaweed
washed up by the tide and baking in the sun. It filled
her with an irrational sense of well-being, nostalgic
for a time she could barely remember.

Jenny trotted across beige sand and hopped onto a
fallen log, bleached white by the sea. She patted the
smooth space next to her. "Sit here, Miz Tory. I want
to talk to you."

Smiling at the serious turn of phrase, Tory sat. The

log was smooth, sun-warmed, a little sandy. "About what?"

"My mother," Jenny said promptly. "I want to talk about my mother."

"Listen, Jenny, I don't think your daddy would like that."

Jenny's frown resembled her father's, too. "The window you're making is for my mommy. I can tell you lots of things that will help." She pointed to the small purple and white flowers blooming close to the ground among the sea oats in the dunes. "See those?"

"Beach morning glories, aren't they?" She hadn't expected to, but she remembered the tiny, trumpet-shaped flowers from those early childhood holidays when her father was alive and the family summered on Tybee Island. Her fingers automatically picked up the pencil.

"Those were my mommy's favorite flowers." Jenny said it firmly, as if to refute argument.

"They're very pretty." Beach morning glories began to grow on the paper under her hand.

"I remember lots of things." A frown clouded her small face. "Like how Mommy smelled, and what she liked to eat. And—"

"What are you doing?"

Tory's heart jolted into overdrive. Adam stood at the end of the path, glaring. There wasn't any doubt that his sharp question was aimed at her.

Chapter Four

A rush of anger threatened to overwhelm Adam. Tory was talking to his daughter about Lila. He clenched his fists. He'd avoided her questions so she'd turned to his child. How dare she?

Jenny's stubborn pout reached through his anger to sound a warning note. Careful. Don't make too much of this in front of her.

"We're talking, Daddy." Jenny tilted her chin. "About Mommy."

"I see." He crossed the sand toward them, put one foot on the bleached log, tried for a casualness he didn't feel. "That's nice, sugar, but Miz Becky's looking for you. She has your snack ready."

"But, Daddy, I don't want to go yet. I'm not done telling Ms. Tory about Mommy."

He pushed down another wave of anger at Tory, took Jenny's hands and swung her off the log.

"Maybe not, but Miz Becky's waiting for you. Get along, now."

Jenny pouted, then glanced at Tory. "I'll see you after a while. We'll talk some more." At his warning look, she darted toward the path.

The smile Tory had for his daughter slipped from her face once Jenny was gone. She planted her hands against the log on either side of her, seeming to brace herself for battle. "Is something wrong?"

"I think you know something's wrong." Anger drove him, so intense he almost didn't know where to begin. "First off, Jenny's not supposed to go to the beach without asking, even with a grown-up."

Tory lifted her level brows. "Miz Becky gave her permission. Surely you don't think I'd take Jenny anywhere otherwise."

"I don't know what you'd do." Being blunt might be the only thing that would work with the woman. "You were probing Jenny for information about her mother." He flung the words at her like missiles. He wanted her to admit she'd been wrong. More than that, he wanted her gone.

She didn't give any sign of being struck. "I wasn't probing. Jenny brought it up. She wanted to talk."

His heart seemed to wince at that, and for a moment there was no sound but the rustle of sea oats bowing in the wind. Then he found his voice. "That's ridiculous. Jenny was only four when her mother died. She barely recalls her."

"Maybe that's the point. She wants to remember."

Passion flared in Tory's face, vivid and startling. "Don't you realize that?"

Her question flicked him on the raw edges of emotion, and he wanted to hit back. "I realize it's none of your business."

Her mouth tightened, as if acknowledging his right to say it. "You can't stop the child from remembering." Her voice softened, and she put up one hand to brush windblown hair from her eyes. "Why would you want to?"

It was safer not to stare into brown eyes that seemed to know too much about loneliness. He looked beyond Tory, focusing on the inexorable movement of the waves rolling into shore. A line of sandpipers rushed importantly along the wet sand. He struggled, trying to find the right words.

"I don't. But I don't want her to be stuck in grieving. Jenny needs to look forward," he said. "There's nothing to be gained by dwelling on the past."

"Are you talking about Jenny or about yourself?" The question was like a blow to the stomach, but before he could react, she was shaking her head. "I'm sorry. I shouldn't have said that."

"No." He had to force the word through tight lips. "You shouldn't." She had no right.

"I just want…" She let the words trail off, then held her sketch pad out to him. "Look. This is what I'm trying to do."

He took the pad, frowning at a sketch of beach morning glories trailing along the page. "You're drawing flowers. What does that have to do with questioning my daughter?''

Tory's sigh was audible. ''I wasn't questioning her. Coming down to the beach was Jenny's idea. She brought me here because she wanted to show me something—the morning glories. She says they were her mother's favorite flower.''

''I don't think so.'' Lila hadn't even like the beach. She'd longed to return to her native Atlanta almost from the day they'd married. The beach was always too windy or too hot or too cold for her.

Tory stood, the movement bringing her close enough that her wiry hair, escaping from its band and caught by the breeze, brushed his arm. ''Look.'' She touched the drawing. ''Don't you see? I could work this into the design for the window.''

''The window.'' Back to that again. Or maybe they'd never left it. ''I told you we'd decided to do the repairs first.''

She wasn't listening to him. Her gaze focused on the pad, and she pulled it from his hands. She sat back on the log as if she'd forgotten he was there, her pencil flying across the paper.

He watched, bemused. Tory had withdrawn into some other world where nothing could touch her. He doubted she heard the screech of the gulls or the rustle of the sea oats. Only the breeze drew a reaction from her as she pushed her hair back impatiently and smoothed the paper flat.

''There,'' she said at last, looking at him, eyes

alight with passion. "See? This is what I can do with it." She thrust the sketch pad at him.

He took it, sitting down next to her on the log. How was he going to get through to the woman if she wouldn't even listen to what he said?

"This is the window's shape." Her finger traced the arched rectangle she'd drawn. "That's a given. The border can go all around."

She'd turned the morning glories into a twining design that made a frame for whatever would go into the center. He didn't want to be intrigued, and he fought the feeling.

"As I said, we want you to do the repairs first. We're not ready to plan the window yet."

Her gaze probed for what lay behind the words. "I know. You've told me, several times. But you don't understand. It takes time to create a new design and order the materials. I have to work on this now, while I'm doing the repairs, or I won't be ready when the time comes."

How did he argue with that? Did he tell her the truth—that she'd never come up with a design he'd approve of because such a thing could never exist?

He concentrated on the page, trying to ignore the wave of energy coming from Tory. But he couldn't do that, either.

This mattered to her. Maybe she brought this kind of passion to all her work. Did she have any of that passion left over for anything or anyone else?

Not a question he had the right to wonder about, he told himself quickly.

"All right." He gave in because he didn't know what else to do, and it didn't really matter, anyway. "This looks fine, although I think Lila preferred hot-house orchids." Now, how had that slipped out? He didn't intend to tell her anything.

Dismay filled Tory's eyes. "But Jenny said her mother loved the morning glories."

He shook his head. "Maybe Jenny's confused. Or it's just her imagination."

She reached out as if to take the pad. "I can change the design."

"No." His grip tightened. "Leave it. It's more important that Jenny feel a part of this project."

Tory's rare smile lit her face, making his breath catch. "That's true. I'm glad you see it that way."

See it that way? What on earth was wrong with him? He didn't want this window. The last thing he should do was encourage Tory. But he had the uneasy feeling her smile could make him forget his decision, if he let it.

What was Adam thinking?

For a few minutes Tory had been totally absorbed in the idea that was taking shape under her fingers. She'd forgotten Adam was next to her.

Now he seemed uncomfortably close, and even through the distraction caused by his physical presence, she knew he was hiding something. Some alien emotion roiled beneath his calm facade. She didn't know what it was, but it had to do with his wife. Lila.

Adam flipped through the sketch pad as if to distance himself from any discussion of the window. She watched his hands move over her drawings and wondered how he'd react if he ever saw the sketch in her old pad from that long-ago summer—the one she'd drawn of him after that night at the yacht club. She'd almost thrown it away a dozen times, but something always stopped her.

He wouldn't see it, she assured herself. He'd obviously forgotten that night, and she'd never remind him. Their relationship was complicated enough without that.

Adam stopped, turned back a page to something he must have missed the first time through.

"When did you do this?" His voice had changed as he tilted the sketch of Jenny toward her. Maybe the current battle was over, if not the war.

"This morning. She looked as if she were trying to go into orbit on that swing."

His lips twitched. "She does do that, doesn't she? She scares me half to death sometimes." He quirked an eyebrow at her, green eyes smiling, and her heart turned over. "May I have this?"

Apparently they'd declared a truce for the moment. "Of course, if you really want it." She felt the heat come up in her cheeks. "It's not that good. I'm not an artist, just a craftsman."

His tanned fingers touched the drawing lightly. "Looks pretty professional to me. Anyway, you caught that sense of adventure in her face. That's wonderful, even when it terrifies me."

"You wouldn't want her to be any different." She

thought about her mother and stepfather, who'd always wanted her to be different. About her grandmother and Jason, who'd have loved her if she'd been willing to change.

"Of course not." He looked surprised, as if the thought had never occurred to him. "Jenny is herself. I wouldn't change her for the world." He smiled. "But I thank God every day that I have plenty of people to help me with her—family, Miz Becky. I don't know what I'd do without them."

"Caldwell Island is filled with Caldwells, isn't it?" And Adam Caldwell belonged here, in a way she'd never belonged anywhere.

"We are kind of thick on the ground," he agreed. He seemed to relax now that they were away from the subject of the window. "Especially since my brother and my cousin Chloe came home. We never thought those two wanderers would settle down. At least, nobody thought it but Gran."

She pictured the erect elderly woman with her obvious pride in her family. "I take it the Caldwell clan was among the first settlers on the island."

"Oh, yes." He stretched, his arm brushing hers and sending a trickle of warmth along her skin. He nodded toward the mainland, shimmering green against the blue water to the west. "The island doesn't seem far from the mainland now, but before the bridge was built, this was wild country. The first Caldwells date back to the eighteenth century, and they lived pretty isolated for a long time."

"Sounds like there's a story in that." She put a

question in her voice. Her mother had said that the carved dolphin was somehow related to the Caldwell family's history. Maybe if Adam talked about it...

He shrugged. "Lots of stories, but I'm not the best one to tell them. Get Gran going on it sometime. She's a real sea island storyteller. Nobody knows the legends like she does."

"I'll bet you know them. After all, you grew up here, while I—"

She stopped that thought before it could spill out, appalled at her carelessness. She'd almost said she'd only been here twice.

"While you?" He smiled, watching her, and her heart seemed to lurch. There was something about his interested gaze that made a person want to confide in Adam. He focused on her with such flattering attention that it drew the words out. Maybe that was why, as Miranda had said, everyone depended on him.

She managed a smile in return. "While I'm a new-comer," she said firmly. "A visitor, isn't that what you'd say? I notice no one says tourist."

"We think visitor sounds nicer. Anyway, we've never had what you'd call hordes of tourists on the island. Just as well, as far as most of us are concerned. Mostly we get the summer residents who own or rent those houses down by the yacht club."

The last place she wanted to discuss was the yacht club. It brought back too many memories—dancing in the moonlight, the scent of white roses, the feel of Adam's strong arm around her waist.

"I understand a new hotel is going up," she said hurriedly.

He nodded, but he seemed distracted, too, as if chasing down a vagrant thought. Because he was recalling a moonlit night that was better forgotten?

"It'll mean changes," he said. "Good or bad, I guess we'll see. More nightlife, probably. Lila would have liked that." He stopped abruptly, as if surprised at his words.

"She enjoyed going out?" Tory was so glad to be off the dangerous topic of the yacht club that she asked the question without thinking.

He snapped the sketch pad closed, and his face closed, too. "Yes." He clipped off the word. "But I don't see how you can incorporate that into your design."

"I wasn't..." *I wasn't trying to get you to talk about her. I just wanted to change the subject.*

Obviously she couldn't say that. Before she could think of something noncommittal, he stood.

"I'd best get back."

He didn't give her a chance to say she'd walk to the house with him. He spun away from her and strode up the path as if something were chasing him.

Memories, she thought. *Memories are chasing you, Adam, and you don't want to let them catch up. Is it because you grieve for your wife so deeply? Or do you have some other reason?*

Well, she was certainly the last person he'd confide in. She tilted her head, letting the breeze tangle her hair. She'd have done a better job of handling that conversation if she hadn't been so worried about her own secrets.

She frowned at the sketch of the beach morning glories. She could create something good from that, if Adam would let her. If.

Where is this going, Lord?

There didn't seem to be an answer.

Tory hadn't, in her wildest imaginings of being on Caldwell Island, expected to be standing next to Adam in the front pew on Sunday morning, sharing a hymnbook as the pastor announced the last hymn. Adam flipped to the song, his hand brown against the white page, and she stilled the by-now-familiar tingle at his nearness.

She'd been startled at his automatic assumption they'd go to church together. When she'd met him at the bottom of the stairs and waited with him for Jenny and Miz Becky, it had been almost as if they were family.

No, not that. She hurried away from that notion and focused instead on the window of Jesus and the children. She and Adam had worked late with his crew the evening before, wanting to put the repaired panels back before this morning.

Last night, she'd felt as if they were on the same team. But they weren't. She had to remember that. She had an undeclared purpose here, and she had the strong feeling that Adam was hiding something, too.

Sunlight slanted through the old glass, casting rays of ruby and amethyst across the faces of the worship-ers. She found herself drawn to the image of Jesus. The light behind the window made the face glow with an inner peace.

You brought me here, she prayed silently. *Show me what to do.*

She had to succeed. The thought sent a shiver through her. Because if she didn't, she'd spend her life thinking she'd failed her mother one last time. She couldn't be in this sanctuary without seeing that shelf and knowing what she had to do.

Show me, she said again. *Please.*

"Eternal Father, strong to save, whose arm has bound the restless wave..." She sang the words with the congregation, sensing the emotion that rippled through the sanctuary. These people lived lives surrounded by the ocean. They knew what it was to beg God's mercy for those in peril on the sea.

Her gaze moved to the dolphin shelf behind the pulpit, filled with the late chrysanthemums Adam's grandmother had put there. Was that why the dolphin had been so important to them—because of its connection with the ocean?

She had to know more. And Adam was the one who could tell her, if he would. If she had the courage to bring it up.

She slanted a sideways glance at him. As if feeling her gaze, he looked at her, eyes crinkling in a smile, and her hand tightened on the hymnal.

The amen sounded, and Pastor Wells lifted his hands. "Before we leave today, I'd like to draw your attention to the window of Jesus and the children. The repair work has already been finished on it, and I'm sure you'll want to say a word to the stained-glass artist who will be with us working on the windows, Tory Marlowe."

He nodded toward her, smiling, and she didn't know where to look. She hadn't expected that. She was here to do a job, not become a part of this community.

Pastor Wells launched into his benediction, and the moment passed. But she soon found that wasn't all there was to it. Once the organist began to play the postlude, everyone in the sanctuary seemed intent on speaking to her.

By the time she'd shaken hands a dozen times, nodded and smiled and said whatever she could about the windows, Adam had slipped away.

Fine, she told herself. She hadn't expected him to wait for her. Not when she was just someone he had to put up with for the duration. She could easily walk to the house.

"You did a fine job with that." Adam's grandmother paused next to her, navy bag clasped in white-gloved hands.

"Thank you." She joined Mrs. Caldwell in looking at the window. "The cleaning really brought out those beautiful colors."

"Always has been one of my favorites." The elderly woman reached up to settle her navy straw hat more firmly. "Which one do you reckon to do next?"

Tory nodded toward the image of Jesus feeding the five thousand. "That one. But I'm not sure I'll have it finished by next Sunday." She frowned, worrying. "If they can get it to me quickly…"

Mrs. Caldwell patted her hand. "You talk to Adam about it. He'll work it out." She moved away.

Talk to Adam. Yes, she'd do that.

And she had to talk to Adam about the dolphin. She traced a glass flower, wondering. Maybe the time had come to level with him about who she was. That might be the only way she'd gain his cooperation. Without that, she stood little chance of finding out what had happened to the dolphin. Still, she couldn't help cringing at the thought of telling him.

"Are you planning your strategy?"

She jumped at the baritone voice so close behind her, her heartbeat accelerating. Adam hadn't gone, after all. Was he reading her mind?

Chapter Five

Tory tried to catch the breath his words had stolen. Adam was in the nearest pew, apparently gathering discarded bulletins. It took a moment to convince herself he wasn't reading her mind. With a wave of relief, she realized he was talking about the window, not her search for the dolphin.

"Something like that. I'd like to get started on the next one." She paused. "I thought you'd already left."

He lifted an eyebrow. "My daddy always told me if you bring a lady somewhere, you take her home again."

"Going to church isn't—" *A date.* She didn't want to say that. "I could easily walk back to the house. It's not far and it's a beautiful day."

Adam nodded, scooping the bulletins into a neat stack. "October weather is perfect on the island. I never have figured out why the visitors don't seem to know that." He grinned. "Not that I'm complaining about it, you understand."

"I can see why you want the place to yourself, if that's what you mean." She glanced around. It was disconcerting to be suddenly alone with him when a few moments earlier the church had been full. "Is Jenny outside?"

"Miz Becky took her on home. She wanted to get started on lunch. The buildings and grounds chair always gets stuck with last-minute chores after the service."

That sounded like an invitation. "Can I help?"

"Sure." He looked around the empty sanctuary as if picking out a job for her. "You might take those flowers from the dolphin shelf. We'll drop them off for one of the shut-ins on our way home."

Tory moved slowly past the pulpit, her gaze on the bracket where the carved wooden dolphin had once stood. She inhaled the spicy aroma of the chrysanthemums, then ran her hand along the shelf. Her fingertips touched the border of seashells, incised by a careful hand generations ago. Someone had put a great deal of love into the shelf to hold the dolphin.

Her throat tightened. The disappearance of the dolphin had messed up several lives. Returning it couldn't erase the damage, but it was the last thing she'd ever do for her mother. Maybe that would make up for all the times she'd failed—failed to understand, failed to keep her mother from drinking again, failed to somehow save her from herself.

"Tell me about the dolphin." She tried to keep her

voice casual, not wanting Adam to guess it meant anything at all to her.

"My gran would tell it better." He shoved a hymnal into the pew rack.

But she wanted to hear it from him. "I'm sure you know it by heart."

"Nobody knows how much truth there is to the story," he warned.

"I'll take it as legend." She smiled, trying to disguise how keyed up she was.

He shrugged, as if giving in to her whim, and leaned his hip against the pew back. "It's said the first Caldwell on the island was a shipwrecked sailor. Supposedly he was close to drowning when an island girl and her dolphins rescued him. 'He took one look and knew he'd love her forever,' that's what Gran always says." Adam's voice deepened on the words. "He carved the dolphin as a symbol of their love. Tradition says those who marry under the dolphin's gaze are especially blessed."

She thought he was moved more than he wanted to admit by the story. Her throat had certainly tightened. He took one look and knew he'd love her forever. What woman didn't long for that, even though she knew it was a fantasy? The silent sanctuary seemed to murmur of the hundreds of vows that had been uttered there.

"What happened to the dolphin?" she asked when she could speak again.

Adam walked toward her, mounting the single step to the chancel. His sleeve brushed her arm as he touched the shelf, and she resisted the urge to step backward. He traced the carving as she had done.

"The carving stood here for generations. My dad was around when it disappeared. He was in his teens then."

I know. "Did they ever find out who took it?"

He was close enough that she could see the change in his eyes at the question. Some strong emotion showed for a moment and was quickly suppressed.

"No." His voice was colorless.

He knew more, she was sure of it. "They must have had some idea."

Adam's hand tightened on the shelf until the knuckles whitened. "There were stories. They say some rich girl—a summer visitor—was involved."

Grief had a stranglehold on her throat, but she forced the words out. "Why would she do that?"

"Who knows? A whim, maybe." He let go of the shelf suddenly, as if he didn't want to touch it while he spoke of it. "Something to do on a lazy summer day. It didn't mean anything to her. Obviously she didn't care what it meant to us."

Contempt filled Adam's voice, and her heart contracted. She'd wanted the dolphin story, and he'd given it to her. But she'd gotten something she hadn't bargained for.

He blamed her mother. She struggled with that unpalatable truth. He apparently didn't know who the rich girl was, but he held her responsible. She should have realized that would be the case. Probably the whole Caldwell clan felt the same way about her mother.

The brief thought she'd had of telling Adam the truth about herself suddenly seemed very foolish. She couldn't. He resented her presence because of the memorial window. If he knew who she was, he wouldn't tolerate her for another instant.

That knowledge hurt more than it had any right to.

He was spending too much time watching Tory, Adam decided. Maybe it was Miz Becky's fault for seating her directly across from him at the dinner table that Sunday evening. How could he help noticing the way the candlelight reflected in Tory's dark eyes and the sheen of her hair against the white dress she wore?

All right, he was drawn to her. He'd already admitted that to himself. And it wasn't just the way she looked. He'd seen the passion in her eyes when she talked about her work and he'd glimpsed her caring heart in the drawing she'd done of Jenny.

Unfortunately the bottom line was that he hated her reason for being here. He'd stop her if he could.

With a spurt of determination, he focused on his father, seated as always at the head of the oval mahogany table. Dad had been talking for the last ten minutes about his latest business trip. A trip that had, as always, been extended so he didn't get back in time for the Sunday service.

Had Tory wondered about his father's absence from worship this morning? Probably not. She hadn't been around long enough to know it was habitual.

He fingered the heavy silver knife, letting it clink against the china plate. Tory also didn't know he hadn't told her the whole truth about the dolphin's disappearance. He hadn't told her the most significant part—that his father had taken it.

Miz Becky's pecan pie turned tasteless in his mouth. Matt had been the one to learn about Jefferson's involvement. According to Matt, Dad claimed he'd borrowed the dolphin to impress a girl. The party they'd been attending was raided, and when all the confusion cleared, he'd never seen either the girl or the dolphin again.

Too many questions remained unanswered about that night—questions Adam had never asked. He'd accepted what his brother told him. He hadn't ever so much as brought it up with his father. Maybe it was time he did.

Adam slanted a glance at his father. Jefferson was being charming to Tory at the moment. The courtly Southern gentleman was a role he liked to play, as if it canceled out the ambitious businessman he really was.

Jefferson picked up his coffee cup. "If you'll excuse me, there are some contracts in the study I must put away."

"I'll join you." Adam's chair scraped as he shoved it back. For a moment he wondered what he was doing. He was the family peacemaker, wasn't he? He was about to stir up trouble. "I need to discuss something with you."

His father lifted an eyebrow slightly, then nodded.

With a murmured excuse to Tory, Adam followed him next door to the study.

The book-lined room was dim and still. His father crossed to the desk where a single brass lamp cast a circle of light. He started shuffling together the papers that littered the surface.

He glanced at Adam. "What is it, son? Something about the boatyard?"

"No." As always, his father's first concern was business. "I've come about the dolphin."

Jefferson's manicured hands froze on the papers, and his face looked old. "You know all there is to know from your brother. I don't see any benefit to discussing it again."

"You talked to Matt about it." At some level, that rankled. Why had Matt—the rebel, the wanderer—been the one his father confided in? Why not him, the good son who'd always been there for his father?

"Only because he didn't give me much choice." His father frowned.

Adam didn't move. After a long moment Jefferson slumped into the leather chair behind the cherry desk. A breeze from the French doors ruffled the papers on the desk and brought the scent of the salt marsh into the room.

"All right," his father said finally. "What are you wondering?"

He'd been holding his breath. He let it out slowly. "I want to know why. Just why. Why did you take the dolphin?"

His father leaned back, rubbing his temples as if to

massage away memories. "I was sixteen. It was a girl. Your brother must have told you that."

"Not just any girl." Why, Dad? Why would you betray everything your family held dear?

"No." The lines in his father's face deepened. "Not any girl. Emily Brandeis."

"A summer visitor."

Jefferson shook his head with sudden impatience. "I can't make you understand what it was like then."

"Try." It might be the first time in his adult life he'd pushed his father.

Jefferson stared at him, his face tightening. "They looked down on us—the yacht club people with their fancy boats and fine houses. They thought we were dirt beneath their feet."

Bitterness etched his father's voice. Was that where his drive to succeed at any cost had come from? "Including the girl?"

"Emily was different." His voice softened. "She was—a golden girl. Different from anyone I'd ever known. It was like having a princess step out of a fairy tale. And she wanted to be with us, Clayton and me."

So Uncle Clayton was part of this story. "The three of you were friends."

"More than that. Puppy love, I suppose it was, but I've never felt anything like it before or since. I'd have done whatever Emily wanted. And when she teased us about getting the dolphin for her—"

He stopped, his lips twisting. "Clayton wouldn't. Mr. Goody Two-shoes would never do anything like that. I wanted to show her I cared for her more that he did. I'd have put it back the next day, and no one the wiser."

Oh, Dad. "You didn't."

"No. We were having a clambake out on Angel Isle. The island kids and some of the summer visitors. We weren't supposed to hang out together, but we did. I showed Emily the dolphin." He stopped.

"And then?" Adam prodded.

His father made a chopping motion as if to cut away the rest of the story. "We quarreled. I left. Later a bunch of yacht club parents raided the party. Emily's father must have been upset that she was hanging out with geechees like us. Her family left the next day."

"That's it?" He sensed things unsaid, things his father would probably never say.

Jefferson's mouth formed a tight line. "Believe it or not, I never saw her or the dolphin again."

Tory took a soundless step away from the open French doors, then another. She backed up until she hit the railing that separated the veranda from the salt marsh. Raising her hand to her cheek, she discovered it was wet with tears.

She hadn't meant to eavesdrop. Their voices had come floating out the open door into the darkness on the veranda. She'd heard her mother's name and she hadn't been able to move away.

Tory wiped tears away with the back of her hand. She couldn't change the past. She had to decide. What was she going to do with the knowledge she'd been hiding?

A footstep sounded, and Adam came through the French doors. The room behind him, lit only by the small desk lamp, was empty. His father must have left while she'd stood there crying. She pressed her hands against the railing, trying to regain control.

Adam took another step, then stopped abruptly. "Tory. I didn't realize you were out here. You look like a ghost in that white dress."

"I'm sorry if I startled you. I came out for a breath of air." To her dismay, her voice was thick with tears.

Adam was at her side in a moment. "What is it? What's wrong?"

She'd asked herself what she should do with her knowledge, but there was really only one possible answer. She had to tell him. But how?

Maybe the only way was to blurt it out.

"I heard you and your father talking."

He stiffened as if she'd struck him. "Eavesdropping, Tory?"

"I didn't mean—" She could hardly claim that. "I'm sorry. I didn't intend to listen."

"Then why did you? You could have walked away." Contempt edged his voice.

She took a breath. She should have known from the beginning that this foolish plan of hers would never work—that she would fail her mother in this, too. "Because you were talking about my mother."

Adam's silence was probably shock.

"Your mother was Emily Brandeis."

"Yes."

The evening was so still she heard the intake of his

breath, caught the faint splash of something moving out in the marsh. Then the breeze picked up again, fanning her hot cheeks and rustling the spartina grass.

"I don't understand." At least there wasn't anger in his voice, not yet. He took a step closer, his hand on the rail, his gaze intent on her face in the dim light. "Did you know the connection when you came here?"

"I knew."

"Why didn't you tell me?" Anger spurted through his words, scalding her.

"I'm telling you now."

"You should have told me the day we met."

Of course he'd think that. "It was all so complicated. What was I supposed to do that first day in the church? Announce that I was here to repair the windows and, by the way, my mother was involved in the disappearance of the dolphin?"

"That would have been better than hiding it from all of us."

"I didn't know enough, don't you understand that?" She wanted to grasp him and make him believe her, but she couldn't. "I had to try and find out where you stood before I could tell you anything."

He shook his head. "This is crazy." Something sharpened in his tone. "Did you talk my mother-in-law into this commission just so you could come here?"

"Of course not." She should have realized he'd assume the worst. "She'd already decided on the window. I had nothing to do with that. But when I saw her ad for someone to work at the Caldwell Cove church, I felt as if it was meant.''

"Meant." He repeated the word heavily. "Why? What possible reason could you have for coming to the island? Don't tell me you've finally decided to give the dolphin back."

Her nails bit into her palms. He'd never believe her, and he'd probably use this as an excuse to stop work on the windows. She couldn't blame him.

"You have to understand." She said the words slowly, hoping against hope he'd hear the truth in them. "I can't give the dolphin back. I don't have it. I never did. My mother didn't take it off the island."

There was silence again, but this time sheer disbelief emanated from him. It hurt more than she'd have thought possible.

"How can I believe that?" Adam flung out his hand toward the study door. "You were listening. You heard what my father said."

"She didn't take it away." She searched for the words that would convince him. "All I can tell you is what I believe to be the truth. When my mother was dying, she seemed to become fixated on that time. It was as if she thought all the problems in her life stemmed from the events of that summer." She couldn't stop the tremor in her voice. "Maybe knowing you're dying does that to a person."

Some of the anger seemed to go out of him at her pain. "I'd forgotten she died so recently." He touched her wrist, his sympathy light as a gull's wing. "I'm sorry."

Her tears tried to surface again, and she fought them back.

"I hadn't known about the dolphin before, but it seemed to haunt her. She kept saying, 'I never meant for him to take it.' I didn't know then who she meant."

"I guess we know now." His voice was dry, but his father's actions had to have cut him deeply. They were both trapped by their parents' behavior.

Her hands clenched. "It doesn't seem to lead anywhere. Your father says he gave her the dolphin. But she didn't take it away."

The clouds cleared from the moon, showing her his face, intent and frowning. To her relief, his antagonism faded as he focused on the problem.

"Didn't she tell you what happened to it?"

She shook her head slowly. It all sounded so improbable, but she knew it was true. "She kept drifting in and out of consciousness those last days. I had to piece it together. One thing was clear—she blamed herself for what happened, but she didn't take the dolphin away."

"How do you know she was telling the truth?" He sounded as frustrated as she felt. "You said yourself she was confused, incoherent."

"She wasn't lying." Tory knew that, bone deep.

"All right, not lying." He frowned, obviously trying to come up with something to explain. "She was just a kid at the time. Maybe she took it, pawned it, even threw it away. Then she was ashamed and didn't want to admit it. Did you look through her papers for any clue?''

"Of course I did. There was nothing.'' She reached out to grasp his sleeve, intent on making him believe her. She could feel the warmth of his skin through the fine cotton, and she had to take a breath before she could go on. "I know she didn't take the dolphin. I know because of what she asked me to do.''

"What do you mean?'' His hand closed hard over hers. "What did she ask you to do?''

He was listening. He wasn't dismissing her out of hand.

"That was my mother's dying wish.'' She forced away the tears she was determined not to shed in front of him. "She begged me to find the dolphin and put it back in the church where it belongs.''

Chapter Six

It was true, then. Adam wanted to reject Tory's words, but he couldn't. Her determined, passionate face convinced him he couldn't deny them, no matter how much he wanted to.

His gaze traced her features, turned toward him in the moonlight. His father had described Emily as a golden girl, but Emily's daughter was the opposite. The dim light silvered her skin, as if she were a pen-and-ink sketch of a woman.

He had to say something. "It's over then. The dolphin is lost for good." His sense of relief surprised him. He'd have said they all wanted it back, but maybe he didn't feel that way. As far as he was concerned, raking up the past only seemed to bring pain. "Now we can stop wondering what happened."

"It's not over." The passion in her voice caught him off guard. "It can't be over."

"Tory—" He shrugged, feeling helpless in the face

of her reaction. "What do you expect to do? The dolphin's been gone for forty-some years. There's no way we can find it now."

You. He should have said *you.* He shouldn't align himself with her.

"There has to be." Tory's lips tightened. "Don't you understand? This was the last thing my mother ever asked of me. I made a promise."

"An impossible promise. It's not your fault if you can't keep it."

"You wouldn't say that if you were the one who'd made it."

"I'd face reality." He couldn't help the exasperation that filled his voice.

"No, you wouldn't." She shook her head, her cloud of black hair flying rebelliously. "I didn't have to know you ten minutes to see what mattered to you. You wouldn't give up if you'd made a promise. Loyalty is too important to you for that."

Loyalty. The word lodged in his heart, and he couldn't speak. How could she know that about him? The thought of Lila flickered through his mind, and he pushed it away. Protecting the memory of the wife who'd betrayed him didn't have anything to do with loyalty. He was doing it for his daughter.

"What I would or wouldn't do isn't the question." He had to fight to maintain a detached tone. "Why did it mean so much to your mother? You'd think she'd have forgotten the dolphin."

Matt had said that Emily Brandeis had died in poverty. What had happened to his father's golden girl?

"She never forgot. That night—I don't know, it was as if something broke in her that night." Tory's eyes clouded with pain, and he fought a ridiculous urge to comfort her. "She felt guilty for involving your father and his brother. Apparently her father was so furious that he took her away the next day. He pushed her into the life he'd planned for her—the right schools, the right friends, the right marriage."

The bitterness with which she said the last words tipped him off. "I take it the marriage wasn't so right, after all."

She shrugged, but the casual gesture couldn't hide her pain. "I don't remember much about my father, but by all accounts it wasn't a happy marriage. She remarried after his death. The situation with my step-father wasn't much better. Maybe it would have lasted a little longer, but the summer we came here—"

She stopped abruptly, her lips tightening as if to keep back the words.

"I thought you'd never been to the island before." Suspicion sharpened his voice. He'd been too quick to believe her.

"I…" She looked at him, maybe considering another lie. Then she shook her head. "I was here once." The words came out reluctantly. "A long time ago, when I was fifteen."

"We met then." His sureness surprised him. He hadn't remembered her before, but now he knew. There'd been that sense of familiarity that plagued him from the first day at the church.

"We met," she agreed. "I came to a dance at the yacht club, and you were there."

He stared at her, memories stirring. The yacht club terrace, music playing in the background, the scent of roses. A girl wearing a white dress, standing in the moonlight.

"You wore a white dress. You had a white rose in your hair."

He thought she flushed, although he couldn't be sure in the dim light. "That's right. It was nothing. Just a dance."

"A dance." He frowned at her, remembering. "You turned into Cinderella, as I recall. You ran off and you didn't bother to leave a glass slipper behind."

Something quick and pained crossed her face. "I had to leave."

"Why?" He wouldn't let her get away with less than the whole story.

"My mother." She looked past him, toward the spartina grass waving in the marsh, but he wasn't sure she saw it. "When I called home to ask if I could stay later at the dance, my mother was crying. Hysterical. I knew what that meant."

A dozen possibilities raced through his mind. "Your stepfather—"

"No, he wasn't abusive, not physically, anyway. But he didn't understand her. When something upset her, she couldn't help it." She seemed to be begging him to understand. Or maybe she was trying to understand herself. "She'd start down into depression. I always thought if I just got to her soon enough, I could stop it. But I never could.''

He saw. "You think it was because she'd come back to the island.''

"I know it was. This place haunted her. I promised I'd put that to rest for her. I have to try.'' Her eyes were wide and dark in the moonlight. "Will you help me?''

If she'd asked him that ten minutes ago, he might have been able to resist. He didn't want to do this.

But he'd seen how much it hurt her. Like it or not, his family shared the responsibility. He couldn't say no.

"All right,'' he said finally. "I don't know what I can do—what either of us can do. But I'll try.''

The smile that blossomed on her face would have made any amount of effort worthwhile. "Thank you, Adam. My mother would be grateful.''

"I'm not doing it for her. I don't even think I'm doing it for you.''

Her brows lifted. "Then why bother, if you don't believe we're going to get the dolphin back?''

He thought about what Tory must have faced when she'd run out of the yacht club that night. Regret shimmered through him. She'd been a kid, and by the sound of it, she'd had to be a parent to her mother. She hadn't deserved that.

"I guess I'm doing it for that girl in a white dress with a rose in her hair,'' he said.

Tory brushed at her hair a little self-consciously. "Maybe I should wear a rose in my hair more often.''

"Maybe you should." He touched the springing hair at her temple. He intended it for the lightest of gestures, a relief from the emotion of the last few minutes.

But a lock of her hair twined around his finger, almost as if clinging to him. He brushed the fine skin at her temple.

"Did I kiss you that night?"

She swallowed, and he felt the effort through his fingertips. "I don't remember."

"Hard to believe I wasn't more memorable than that." He tried to keep it light, but something deeper than memory was driving him. "Maybe we should try it again."

"I'm not sure—"

He stopped her words with his kiss. Her eyes closed. He made no move to hold her, and nothing touched but their lips. It should have been the simplest of gestures.

A wave of longing swamped him. He wanted that feeling again—wanted to see the future stretching ahead of him, ready to be explored, clean as a fresh page in Tory's sketch pad.

But he couldn't have that again. Probably neither of them could. He drew back reluctantly, not quite able to regret that he'd kissed her.

"I guess I should apologize."

Tory shook her head quickly. "It's all right. It doesn't mean anything."

She spun and hurried toward the door, the white

dress fluttering in the evening breeze. In an instant she was gone.

There was no fresh page. They couldn't go back and become teenagers kissing in the moonlight again. Too much had happened to both of them.

He'd committed himself to helping her in an undoubtedly futile attempt. He'd try, but somehow he didn't think any of this was going to turn out the way Tory wanted. And he couldn't disregard the sense that they were headed for trouble.

Each time she thought about the night before, Tory's stomach tightened. It was a wonder she'd been able to eat any of the mouthwatering she-crab soup Miz Becky had fixed for lunch.

She frowned at the sketch pad in her lap. She'd been sitting in the bentwood rocker on the front veranda since lunch. It was certainly safer to sit here than on the side of the house overlooking the salt marsh. There, she'd have been reminded with every breath of confiding in Adam. Of kissing Adam.

Her stomach quivered as she saw Adam's face in the moonlight. She felt the featherlight touch of his lips, and a wave of longing swept through her. If only—

No. She drowned the longing with anger, but it was anger at herself, not Adam. She'd wasted too many dreams over the years on the Adam she remembered. She wouldn't do that to herself again. She set the rocker moving with a push of her feet. Its creak was oddly comforting. She could be rational about the situation with Adam.

He'd promised his help. That was all she wanted. Other than that, their relationship was strictly business, nothing more.

She was still staring at the page a half hour later when she heard the crunch of tires on the shell-covered driveway. Adam was back from the boatyard, and she hadn't accomplished a thing. She smoothed the cover of the pad over the design.

He came toward her, his step assured, giving her that endearing smile as he mounted the front steps. Her stomach quivered again.

"Hey, Tory." He glanced at the pad in her lap. "Are you busy?"

"Not terribly," she said cautiously. If he brought up last night…

"Come for a ride with me, then. There's something I want to show you."

Her preservation instincts told her that being alone with Adam in a car was not a good idea. "What is it?"

He lifted an eyebrow, the effect devastating. "Don't you like surprises?"

"No." She didn't have to think about that one. All the surprises in her life had been unpleasant ones.

He studied her for a moment, then nodded as if he understood. "All right. No surprises. I was able to find the house your mother's family rented when they came here that summer. I thought you'd want to see it."

She had to catch her breath. He'd promised to help,

but she hadn't expected anything so concrete already. "That was fast."

"It wasn't that hard. There's only one rental agency that handles houses suitable for wealthy summer visitors. Their records go back a hundred years." He nodded toward the car. "Shall we go?"

Tension gripped her, but she couldn't back out. She dropped the sketch pad on the rocker as she stood. "Am I dressed all right?"

"Since I have the keys and no one is renting it, you won't meet anyone but me." His gaze swept her chinos and cotton sweater with what seemed to be approval. "And you look good to me."

Warmth flooded her cheeks. She really hadn't been asking for a compliment. "Let's go, then."

She followed him to the car. He opened the door and took her arm to usher her in. Her skin tingled where he touched it.

Stop it, she lectured as he went to the other door and slid behind the wheel. Just stop it.

Adam turned the car, swung out through the pillared wrought-iron gates to the road, and Caldwell Cove spread out in front of them. From Twin Oaks, situated at the end of the village, a crescent of houses and shops faced the inland waterway. The docks, busy with boats, fringed the water.

Tory's gaze traced the outline of the village, bisected neatly by the church spire, and her fingers itched for her pencils. If she didn't include the few cars along the street in a sketch, the scene might have been today or a century ago.

Adam turned away from town onto the road that swung around the heel of the island. The breeze through the open window freshened as they drove along the shore, lifting her hair. Unfortunately it couldn't blow away the lump that had formed in her throat.

"You're sure you found the right house?" She asked the question more for the sake of saying something than because she doubted him.

"Positive." He glanced at her, creases forming between his brows. "Having second thoughts?"

"No." She couldn't. "But there won't be anything left to find there after forty years."

Adam shrugged, frowning at the narrow road. "I don't expect to find anything, period. Not after all this time. But I said I'd help, and this was the only place I could think of to start."

"I guess you're right." She discovered she was watching his hands on the wheel and averted her eyes as if afraid he'd catch her. "I was so worried about getting here that I didn't spend a lot of time thinking about how I'd look for the dolphin."

That sounded stupid, and she half expected him to say so. Instead he pointed toward the waves. "Speaking of dolphins, there they are now."

She followed the direction of his hand. At first she saw nothing but ocean. Then a silver crescent arced through the waves, followed by another and another. She couldn't stop a gasp. "They're beautiful."

"Yes." His voice was soft. "Seeing them is just as exciting the hundredth time as it is the first."

She glanced at him, moved by the tenderness in his voice. "You said the legend was that the dolphins saved the shipwrecked sailor. Can that part of it possibly be true?"

"Sure. There are plenty of stories about dolphins interacting with people."

"I've seen trained ones, but in the wild, that has to be different."

Adam smiled. "You should see my cousin Chloe. She'd make a believer out of you. She talks to them, and when you watch them, you're convinced they talk back to her."

Adam spoke easily, without the tension that had marked every conversation they'd had since she came to the island. Her gaze followed the dolphins as they headed toward the open ocean. If she could talk to them like his cousin Chloe, she'd thank the dolphins for that.

Adam turned into a shell-covered drive opposite a deserted stretch of beach. The car bounced over ruts, then came to a stop. "There it is."

She looked, and everything in her froze. She was still sitting, hands pressed against the dashboard, when he came around and opened the door.

"Tory? Is something wrong?"

She turned her head slowly, forced herself to focus on his face. "You're sure this is the right house? The one my grandfather rented when my mother was a girl?"

"Of course." He looked puzzled. "Why?"

She swallowed hard. "Because this is also the house my stepfather rented when I was fifteen."

She watched him absorb that, his face troubled.

"It's not so unusual, when you stop to think about it," he said finally. "There are only so many houses of this size to rent now, and there were even fewer then." His gaze rested on her face, sympathetic. "Are you sure you want to go in?"

She wouldn't be a coward about this. "Yes."

They went up the steps to the porch, and Adam put the key in the lock. She looked around, trying to remember their arrival that summer. She couldn't. That had been wiped out by the way the vacation ended.

But she had probably run up the steps, excited and happy at the prospect of staying at the shore. The weathered gray shingles would have been the same, as well as the beach roses climbing the porch rail.

Adam pushed open the door, then looked at her, eyes questioning. "Okay?"

She nodded. "I'm fine." She took a breath and walked into the house.

He followed her to the hallway, then went into the living room, footsteps echoing on the uncarpeted floor. "I'm sure it's been refurnished since you were here."

"Yes." She stood in the archway, scanning the room. New furniture, fresh paint, different pictures on the walls. It was a pretty room, with its pale walls and floral upholstery. Nothing was left of the past.

But the view from the large windows was familiar. She'd stood in the archway looking at her mother sobbing on the sofa and her stepfather shouting in anger and frustration.

"They'd have replaced the mirror." The words came out before she thought about them. "He threw a glass at it and broke it."

Adam touched her shoulder—a brief, sympathetic stroke of his hand. "I'm sorry."

"It's all right." She took a breath, sought for calm.

"How long did you stay?" He was probably trying to help her by talking.

"Just a few days. I remember my mother was brittle, too excited, almost feverish the whole time." She shook her head. "I should have known something was wrong. I shouldn't have gone out that night."

"You were a kid." The anger in his voice startled her. "It wasn't your responsibility."

"I was all she had." She pressed her fist against her stomach as if that would push away the sick feeling of remembering. "I guess I understand now."

"What?" He moved a step closer, as if he wanted to protect her.

But she didn't need protecting. She'd been taking care of herself all her life.

"Why that trip sent my mother over the edge. It's affecting me, being here, and I'm strong. She was fragile. She was always fragile. Being back in the same house, being flooded by memories and guilt— it's not surprising she fell apart. We never should have come here. She didn't want to, but my stepfather didn't listen. He never did."

It was so quiet she heard the intake of his breath. "What happened? After that, I mean."

She tried to concentrate—to separate what really happened then from what she'd learned later. "She was hospitalized for depression, I know. And my stepfather filed for divorce. I stayed in his house until she got out of the hospital, but then I found a place for the two of us."

"You were too young for that." Again there was suppressed anger in his voice. "Wasn't there any family who could help you? What about your father's family?"

"They'd washed their hands of us a long time before that. We did all right on our own."

"You shouldn't have had to."

She tried to force a smile. "Ancient history. It doesn't matter anymore."

She'd never told anyone most of what she'd poured out to Adam. She saw why Miranda said he was everyone's friend. That sympathetic voice had pulled far more out of her than she'd intended to say.

"Well." She tried to sound brisk. "Shall we take a look at the rest of the house?"

He shrugged. "If you want." He studied her face for a long moment. "Are you sure you're okay?"

"Fine." Despite Adam's sympathy, she knew he had his own agenda in all of this. She had to remember that. His family was involved, too.

"You know, it's funny," he said slowly, his gaze still fixed on her face.

"What is?"

"The way things ended, both times. It almost seems as if history repeated itself."

Something shivered inside her. Her mother had been snatched away from her summer love in traumatic circumstances, and she'd never really stopped regretting that.

Years later, Tory had been snatched away just as suddenly.

Nonsense, she told herself sternly. The two things had little in common. Adam hadn't been a summer love. She'd only known him for a single evening. He didn't mean anything to her.

You dreamed about him for years, a little voice whispered in her mind. *How long will you dream about him when you leave this time?*

Chapter Seven

Tory hadn't shaken off the feelings roused by their visit to the beach house when she entered the dining room that night. Being in this place didn't help. Each time she entered the gracious room with the rice-carved mahogany furniture that was unique to the low country, she was reminded of that other life, just as the rice carving was reminiscent of the rice plantations that had once thrived here.

The mahogany-framed mirror over the sideboard reflected her pale face at her. Paler than usual? She wasn't sure.

"Tory." Jefferson Caldwell rose from his seat and pulled out her chair before Adam could move. "Good evening."

She slipped into the chair, glancing at Jefferson's urbane face as he resumed his seat at the head of the oval table. Adam must have told him who she was. What did he think about having the daughter of the woman he'd once been infatuated with in his house? Her tension jerked up a notch. Was this going to be unpleasant?

Jenny bounced into her chair. "Is it my turn to say the blessing?"

Adam nodded, and Jenny lowered her head and clasped her hands. She raced through the words so quickly Tory barely got her head bowed in time. When she looked up, Adam was frowning at his daughter.

"Jennifer Ann, I don't believe that's an appropriate way to ask the blessing. You sound as if you're in a race to get finished."

She wiggled. "But Daddy, you know cousin Andi's coming to spend the night tonight. I want to be done with supper when she gets here so we can play."

"You know perfectly well that Andi will wait if you're not finished with your meal."

"But, Daddy…"

Miz Becky pushed through the door from the kitchen carrying a steaming platter of fried chicken. Tory suspected the distraction was well timed, before Jenny managed to talk herself into any more trouble with her father.

Jefferson offered her a bowl of sweet potatoes. "Andi is my son Matthew's oldest girl," he said, as casually as if explaining his family to any stranger instead of to an interloper who'd hidden her identity from him. "These two young ladies will be giggling all night if we don't watch out."

Jenny looked up from her drumstick. "We'll be good, Grandpa. Honest."

He smiled indulgently at the child. "We'll believe that when we see it. Or when we don't hear it, as the case may be."

Tory was still smiling at Jenny's expression when Jefferson turned to her. "Adam has told me about your mother."

She nearly choked on the sweet potatoes. What was he going to say? He couldn't be happy with the situation. She put her fork down carefully on the silver-trimmed edge of the plate.

"I was sorry to hear of her passing." The words were formal, but sorrow touched his face. "I remember her well."

"Thank you." She hesitated, wondering if she should say more. "She remembered you, too. She... she regretted what happened."

He nodded gravely, his white hair glistening in the light from the chandelier. "I appreciate knowing that, Tory. I wish—" He stopped. "Well, there's little point in revisiting the past." The lines of his face deepened, making him look very different from the young man her mother had talked about.

Did his words mean Adam hadn't told him she wanted to recover the dolphin? She couldn't imagine he'd welcome that. He'd apparently kept his involvement secret for most of his life. She glanced toward Adam for a cue.

He seemed to pick up instantly on her unspoken question. "My father doesn't feel there's much hope of finding it after all these years."

He shot a look toward his daughter, and Tory understood. He didn't want to talk about this in front of her.

"Finding what, Daddy?" Jenny, of course, had picked up on what he might want her to miss.

"Nothing, honey. It's just something that was lost a long time ago."

"I lost my green barrette on the playground last week, and Andi helped me find it. She's good at finding things."

"It sounds as if you're lucky to have a cousin like her," Tory said. Obviously she never should have said anything at the dinner table. Still, Jefferson had been the one to bring it up.

The doorbell rang, and Jenny leaped from her seat. She bounced up and down on her toes, fingertips resting on the edge of the table "That's Andi. May I be excused, Daddy? Please?"

He looked from her half-finished plate to her excited face and sighed. "All right, go ahead. I expect Miz Becky's going to have a snack for you two later."

Jenny darted from the dining room before he finished the sentence, and her high voice echoed from the hallway as she greeted her cousin.

"I'm sorry." Tory glanced from one male Caldwell to the other. "I shouldn't have discussed the subject in front of her."

Jefferson's face darkened with sudden emotion. "Sometimes I wish we'd never heard of that dolphin. We'd be better off forgetting the thing ever existed, legend or no legend."

Well, she'd wondered what he thought. She couldn't blame him for telling her.

"I'd like to forget it, but I can't." She met his gaze squarely. "I made a promise to my mother, and I have to try and fulfill it, even if it seems hopeless." She tensed, waiting for him to suggest she pack her bag.

"Hopeless is the right word. Everything about that situation is hopeless." For an instant Jefferson looked startled at his own emotion. Then he tossed his napkin on the tablecloth. "Excuse me." He went quickly out of the room.

She bit her lip. Her return to Caldwell Cove seemed destined to bring nothing but grief. "I'm sorry. I didn't mean to upset him."

"Forget it." Adam managed a smile, but she could see his tension in the way his hand gripped the fork. "You had to tell him the truth."

"I could have been more tactful. I'm not very good at that." At least it didn't look as if she'd be kicked out. Yet.

"It's all right, Tory."

But it wasn't, and they both knew it. Too many emotions swirled, and no matter what she did, somebody was going to be hurt.

This was what she needed, Tory decided the next morning. A few hours away from anybody named Caldwell and from all the complications associated with their mutual past. She walked down the narrow main street of Caldwell Cove, enjoying the breeze off the water and the salt tang of the air. It was cooler today, with just a hint that autumn must come, even here. She zipped the light windbreaker she'd thrown on when she left the house.

The channel between the island and the mainland was busy with boats of all sizes and descriptions. An elegant sailboat skimmed past a bulky shrimper that drew in toward the public dock. Gulls swooped around it, probably hoping for lunch.

Glancing away from the water, she saw canopies dotting the open lawn between the bank and the café. A few feet closer and she could read the sign. Gullah Market Today.

She hesitated. She ought to get to work, but the windows weren't going anywhere, and she deserved a break. She stepped off the sidewalk and started down the grassy space between the canopies.

Booths offered everything from fresh fruit to baskets to brightly woven cloth. She turned toward the display of baskets and found herself standing next to Miranda Caldwell.

"Hey, Tory. Nice to see you. How are the windows coming along?"

So much for her assumption that she could avoid the sprawling Caldwell clan anywhere in Caldwell Cove. At least it wasn't Adam.

"Fine, thanks. I was ready for a break from them."

Miranda's green eyes sparkled with amusement. "Same here. My mother announced it was time for fall cleaning at the inn, so I decided I needed to come to market."

"These baskets are lovely." Tory picked one up,

hoping it would be a safe subject of conversation. Adam had told his father who she was. Had he passed the information on to the rest of his family? She hoped not.

She probably should have asked him, but things had been strained enough between them after that uncharacteristic display of emotion from his father.

"Sweetgrass," Miranda said, touching the intricately woven strands of the basket. "This is Josepha Green's work. She's a local Gullah basket weaver."

"How can you tell?" Her artisan's curiosity won out over her desire to end the conversation quickly.

"Every Gullah weaver uses the same tools and techniques that have been used for hundreds of years, but each one has his own little trick." She traced the rim of the basket. "See this strand of bulrush woven in? Nobody else does that."

"The artist's personal touch. I guess each of us wants to put our own stamp on things."

"Yes." Miranda's voice was soft. "Like you with your window design, trying to find a way to say who Lila was."

Startled, she met Miranda's gaze, oblivious to the moving, colorful crowd around them. Was she imagining it or was that a hint that Miranda would talk about Lila?

Before she could find a response, someone stopped close behind them. Her pulse thudded, notifying her that it was Adam even before she turned.

"Sharing secrets, ladies?" His words were casual, his eyes guarded. She didn't think he liked finding her in conversation with his cousin.

"Just talking about baskets, sugar." Miranda

smiled. "What brings you away from the boatyard in the middle of the day?"

He shrugged. "The chance I'd run into my favorite cousin talking to Tory, maybe."

She studied him as he bantered with Miranda, switching between English and Gullah, the mixture of dialect native to the sea islands. He should look casual and relaxed in his khakis and faded denim shirt. But the tension lines around his eyes gave him away.

Why didn't he want her to talk to Miranda? Was he afraid of what Tory might say or what Miranda might tell her?

Before she could decide, he turned to her. "If you're done here, I'll give you a ride to the house."

"Sugar, she hasn't even bought anything yet." Miranda linked arms with Tory, her voice gently teasing. "What's wrong? Don't you want to turn your guest loose at market with me?"

"I probably should be getting back to work." Tory felt vaguely uncomfortable, as if she'd been caught gossiping on the boss's time.

"Come on, now," Miranda coaxed. "My daddy's back at the food stand munching on sweet-potato fries. Let's join him."

Adam frowned, and she could feel his tension. "Miranda, if Tory wants to get back to work—"

"Here comes Gran," Miranda interrupted, turning to greet the erect elderly woman who marched toward them through the crowd, nodding or speaking to practically every person there.

Tory took advantage of Miranda's momentary distraction to speak to Adam. "Is there some reason you don't want me to talk with your cousin?" she said quietly.

"Of course not. Why would there be?"

If that were true, he probably wouldn't have spent so much time on his answer. But there was no chance to discuss it. Mrs. Caldwell had reached them.

She zeroed in on Tory. "Miz Tory, you're just the person I want to see. Are you coming to the beach picnic tonight?"

Tory blinked. "I'm sorry. I didn't know about it." Was this something someone had mentioned and she'd forgotten?

Mrs. Caldwell poked Adam's arm. "Well, young man? Why haven't you invited Tory to the picnic yet?"

He caught his grandmother's hand in his. "Stop poking me, Gran. I'm not six anymore. Next you'll be asking if I've brushed my teeth and said my prayers."

His light answer didn't disguise his annoyance. From the sharp look she gave him, it didn't fool his grandmother, either. She turned to Tory.

"Since this grandson of mine didn't remember, I'll do the inviting. The Caldwells are having a picnic on the beach tonight. We want you to come."

She could practically feel Adam willing her to say no. "I don't think I…"

"No excuses, now. You come along with Adam and Jenny, you hear? I'll see you there."

She made it sound like a command. Tory seemed to have no choice but to nod agreement.

But when she looked from Adam's face to his grandmother's she knew she wasn't imagining things. Mrs. Caldwell wanted her there. Adam didn't. He couldn't very well say so, but taking her to this family event was the last thing he wanted to do.

Thanks to Gran, he didn't have a choice about the picnic. Adam paused in the kitchen to pick up the cooler Miz Becky had left ready on the table. He'd best collect Jenny and Tory and be on his way.

His father wouldn't be going, of course. As usual, Jefferson had found a pressing business meeting that took priority. Any other time, Adam might have tried to talk him into going, but with Tory there…

Balancing the family's need to have the dolphin back against Tory's promise and his father's wishes wasn't just difficult—it was impossible. All his instincts told him that having Tory attend the picnic was a bad idea.

As he swung the cooler off the table, he heard the low murmur of voices from the back porch. He moved quietly to the screen door. Tory and Jenny sat on the top step, probably waiting for him.

"Well, I think it was mean." Jenny's pout was visible from where he stood. "Andi didn't have to go home yet. I wanted to play some more."

"If her mother needed her, she probably had to listen." Tory was clearly trying to be the voice of reason for his strong-willed little daughter.

"Her mama would have let her stay if she'd asked. I wanted to cut out paper dolls, but Andi didn't. So she went home. And I'm not going to play with her anymore."

Knowing Jenny's habit of trying to boss everyone around, he suspected there was more to it than that.

He should intervene, but she'd chosen to confide in Tory, not in him.

"Well, I've never had a cousin, so I don't really know what that's like," Tory said. "But I do know what it's like when somebody you love disappoints you."

"It's mean," Jenny burst out, and he realized she was on the verge of tears.

"I'll bet Andi didn't intend to be mean. Of course, sometimes we can hurt other people's feelings even when we don't mean to."

Something about Tory's words must have caught Jenny's attention. She was looking at Tory's face, her resentment seeming to slip away.

"I wouldn't do that," she said self-righteously.

Tory smiled at his daughter with such gentleness it clutched his heart. "I know you wouldn't want to. But don't you think sometimes it happens anyway?"

Jenny's lower lip came out. "Maybe."

"Maybe," Tory agreed. "It isn't easy to forgive someone you love when they've hurt you." She touched the front of Jenny's T-shirt. "But I bet you'll feel better in here if you do. I know when I hold on to being mad at someone, it hurts me more than it does them."

The soft words reached inside him and grabbed his heart in a vise. From the little he'd learned of her family in the last few days, he knew Tory had plenty of reasons to hold on to resentment against them. Apparently she'd found a way to let that go.

Jenny rubbed the front of her shirt. "You mean it makes my heart hurt when I'm mad at someone?"

Tory nodded, lips curving in a smile. "Don't you think you might be able to forgive Andi if you tried?"

Jenny seemed to ponder that. Finally she heaved an elaborate sigh. "Well, I guess it would be more fun at the picnic if we weren't being mad at each other."

"That's a very sensible way to look at it," Tory said solemnly. She touched Jenny's curls lightly. "I'm glad you see it that way."

Forgiving. Adam leaned against the kitchen counter, not quite willing to join them. It was probably just as well Jenny hadn't come to him for advice on that particular subject. It wasn't one he'd dealt with very successfully.

His father and Uncle Clayton hadn't forgiven each other for the differences between them. He couldn't forgive Lila for what she'd done to him and to Jenny. The truth seemed to be that his side of the family wasn't very skilled at forgiving.

And Tory's presence, no matter how he looked at it, seemed to make that worse.

Chapter Eight

"I don't think I should be here." Tory followed Adam and Jenny down the path toward the beach, her footsteps making no sound on the carpet of pine needles. Her sense of not belonging grew stronger by the minute. Adam didn't want her here. She knew that even if he'd never say it.

"Why not?" She detected a faint note of frustration as he switched the cooler he carried from one hand to the other. "My grandmother invited you. Look, they've already started the fire for the crab boil."

They emerged from the shadow of the pines to the dunes, and Jenny darted toward the group gathered on the beach. Some people fed a fire while others unpacked hampers. Children bicycled around them on the hard-packed sand, looking like so many seabirds darting in and out. The orange glow of the fire matched the orange sunset to the west, over the mainland. It was a beautiful, peaceful scene. She didn't belong.

Tory tried to find the words for her uneasiness. "It's a family thing. I'm sure your grandmother just invited me because I'm staying at Twin Oaks."

Adam stopped and smiled at her, the sun lines around his eyes crinkling. Whatever reservations he had about this, he was managing to suppress them. "You don't know my grandmother very well if you think that. Relax, Tory. You'll have a good time."

A good time? She wasn't so sure of that. But maybe it could be a useful time. Adam had said his aunt and uncle would be at the picnic with the rest of their family. This might be her best chance to talk to Clayton about the dolphin.

She'd heard Jefferson's version of events. She wanted to hear Clayton's. Maybe she also wanted to have a glimpse of her mother through his eyes. Did he perceive Emily the same way Adam's father did?

She glanced at Adam, who was lifting his hand to wave to the group on the beach. He belonged to this place and these people. With his faded jeans and his white sweatshirt, he looked like what he was—a man who worked hard, played hard and was at peace with his world.

Or was he? The only chink in his facade was his relationship with his late wife, and that she had yet to figure out. After ten days of working on the sanctuary windows and living in Adam's house, she was no closer to understanding the woman she was supposed to memorialize. Adam wasn't just reticent about Lila—he was a blank wall.

They reached the hard-packed sand where walking was easier, and she paused to shake the loose sand from her shoes. Adam paused, too, looking at her with a hint of a frown in his eyes.

"There's something I should mention before we join the others."

She found herself tensing. The feeling couldn't be shaken off the way the sand could. "What?"

He hesitated, as if wondering how to say whatever it was, and her tension doubled.

"I've told them who you are," Adam said. "They know you're Emily's daughter."

She froze, staring at him, hoping she'd heard wrong. "You what?"

His face tightened. "They're my family. It wasn't something I felt I could keep secret from them. After all, they all know about the dolphin."

"You might have warned me before this." Anger sharpened the words. She should have known he'd tell them. All that loyalty of his was directed toward his family, not her.

"Would you have come if I had?" His gaze challenged her.

"Probably not, but I think I had the right to decide for myself."

"Look, you may as well get used to the situation. No one here is going to blame you for—" He stopped as if realizing where he was headed.

"For something my mother did?" Her fists

clenched so hard her nails bit into her palms. "My mother didn't take the dolphin."

"No." Something bleak appeared in his eyes. "My father did."

"But everyone thinks she took it away. You said so yourself."

He put the cooler down and stood looking at her. Was that sympathy or pity in his eyes? She didn't welcome either. "That was before you told me what she asked you to do. I believe you."

"Do they?" She jerked a nod toward the others, still out of earshot.

"I can't answer that." His jaw tightened as if in exasperation, a small muscle twitching. "You asked me to help you. I'm trying to."

She wanted to flare out at him—wanted to tell him she didn't need his help.

Unfortunately that wasn't true. She did need his help, and she needed the cooperation of those people around the fire. The question was, how likely were they to cooperate with the daughter of the woman they blamed for the disappearance of their family heirloom?

"All right." She bit off the words. "It's too late to change that now. Maybe since your uncle already knows who I am, it will be easier for me to speak with him about that night."

"My uncle—" Adam's expression froze. "I don't think that's necessary."

She blinked. "But he's the only one who might have some clues as to what happened after your father left the party."

"Don't you think my uncle would have spoken up years ago if he did?"

She could hear the anger under his words, but she didn't understand it. "Look, don't you see that this is the next logical step? And there must be other people who were there that night we can talk with."

Adam planted his hands on his hips. "You've already heard my father's account," he said stubbornly. "As for other people—everyone on the island knew by the next day that the dolphin was missing. If they knew anything, they'd have spoken up."

Suddenly she knew what was going on here and why Adam hadn't invited her to this event. He wanted to keep her away from his uncle.

"This is because of the feud between your father and your uncle, isn't it?"

His expression got even more forbidding. "What if it is?"

"I thought you said that didn't affect your relationship with the rest of the family."

She saw the anger flare in his eyes, saw him fight it and control it.

"Fine." He ground out the word. "You want to talk to Clayton, go ahead and do it. Talk to anyone you want. I can't stop you." He picked up the cooler, dangling it from one strong hand. "Let's go." He stalked toward the fire.

Tory followed him, her stomach quivering as they approached the others. That unexpected quarrel with Adam had shaken her confidence, and the fact that everyone was watching them didn't help.

No, not them. Everyone watched *her,* with expressions she could only call guarded. Tension tightened her muscles until it took an effort to walk naturally.

They came up to the cluster of people. For a moment no one spoke. Adam's cousins stopped feeding the fire. His nieces and nephews stopped circling. Everyone looked at her.

Then his grandmother marched toward them.

"'Bout time you two were getting here. You don't want to miss the food, do you? Tory, I'm right glad you decided to join us."

Tory's tension ebbed in the warmth of the elderly woman's smile. "Thank you for inviting me, Mrs. Caldwell."

"Might as well call me Gran. Everyone else does. Make yourself at home. If you don't know somebody, just ask. They all know who you are."

Tory looked for malice in that last sentence but found none in Gran's sharp old eyes. She took a deep breath. She may as well put her cards on the table.

"I understand Adam told you who my mother was."

The elderly woman nodded. "Can't say I'd have recognized you otherwise. You don't favor your mother much, do you?"

The casual question knocked her off balance. She'd forgotten that Adam's grandmother would probably have seen her mother during that long-ago summer.

"No, I guess I take more after my father." That much was easy to say. The next question wasn't. "Did you know her?"

"Not to say *know.* I knew who she was."

Of course she would. Of all the people here, Naomi Caldwell had the most cause to blame Tory's mother for what happened to her sons.

But Adam's grandmother didn't seem to be carrying any resentment. She nodded toward Adam's uncle, bending to put a piece of driftwood onto the fire. "I reckon Clayton's the one you need to see."

Tory felt Adam's tension as surely as if they were touching instead of inches apart. He didn't welcome the idea from his grandmother any more than he'd welcomed it from Tory. Would he tell Gran so?

"Guess I'll go help with the fire," he said, and moved off quickly.

Obviously he wouldn't.

Tory looked at Clayton Caldwell. The lean, gray-haired man walked around the fire, limping slightly. He hadn't so much as glanced in her direction, and her heart sank. "It doesn't look as if Clayton wants to talk to me."

Mrs. Caldwell frowned toward her son, then transferred her gaze to Adam as she assessed each of them. "We don't always get to do what we want to do. Besides, seems to me that this family's been keeping too many secrets for too many years. Secrets aren't good for anyone. That's the verse I gave Adam, you know."

Tory felt as if she'd missed a step in the dark. "Verse?"

The elderly woman shook her head. "Forgot you wouldn't know about that. All my children and grandchildren—the Lord gave me scripture verses for them when they were baptized. Adam's is from Ephesians. 'Speaking the truth in love…'" She paused, looking expectantly at Tory.

Tory was irrationally glad she didn't have to disappoint. "We will in all things grow up into Him who is the head."

That earned her an approving nod. "Maybe it's time for some truth speaking. Maybe that's why you're here." She patted Tory's arm as if she were one of the grandchildren who'd done well.

The touch was disarming. Tory felt a ridiculous urge to pour out all her concerns—about her mother, about Adam, about fulfilling her promise. She pushed the sensation down with a spurt of something like panic. She didn't confide in people. She didn't lean on people. That wasn't how she was.

"I hope you're right." She managed to speak.

Mrs. Caldwell patted her arm again. "Looks like Adam's filled a plate for you. You go on and have your food now. You'll have a chance to hear Clayton's story. Don't you worry about it. He'll get together with you before the evening's over."

She could only hope the woman knew what she was talking about. Mrs. Caldwell walked off, calling the children to come and eat, and Adam approached her, a laden plate in each hand.

"Sorry. Guess I overreacted. Did Gran make everything okay?"

She took the plate he held out to her. "Well, she convinced me that the family isn't planning to run me out of town on a rail, if that's what you mean."

Adam's face relaxed. "Gran's good at reassuring people. Among lots of other things." He took her arm. "Looks like there's room on that blanket. Come and meet my brother and his family."

She let him steer her toward a place to sit. If Adam wanted to make up for his hasty words, she would let him. As she'd told Jenny, it didn't pay to hold a grudge.

The man she knew was his brother looked up at their approach. He smiled and pulled a chubby blond toddler onto his lap to make room for them.

All right, the Caldwells were more welcoming than she had any reason to expect. Apparently Adam hadn't ruined things by telling them about her, but he still should have asked her first. As far as talking to his uncle was concerned, she probably couldn't count on Adam to help her with that.

A question of loyalty, she thought again, glancing at his face as he exchanged banter with his brother. With Adam, things would always come down to that. She knew perfectly well that his loyalty would never be directed to her.

Adam put down his dessert plate and leaned back on his elbows on the blanket. The warmth of the sand lingered even though it was getting dark.

Who'd have guessed he'd find such enjoyment in a family picnic with Tory Marlowe sitting next to him? He watched her lean over to tickle the baby who sat on his sister-in-law's lap. Tory, prickly and uncomfortable at first, had thawed under the influence of

Sarah's warm interest. Sarah seemed to have that effect on everyone. She'd certainly warmed up his brother, turning Matthew from a globe-trotting loner into a contented family man.

It was Sarah who'd produced a windbreaker for Tory to put on. Adam should have thought to warn her it would get chilly after the sun went down. In Sarah's Pirate Days jacket, she looked like a real islander.

Adam looked from one familiar, fire-lit face to another. The children had settled onto blankets around the fire, the younger ones drifting off to sleep, the older ones pointing out constellations in the star-studded sky or toasting one last marshmallow. Jenny huddled close to Andi, their quarrel apparently forgiven and forgotten, as Adam's cousin David started to play the guitar. Under cover of the music he leaned close to Tory.

"I see Uncle Clayton's gone over on the dock to smoke his pipe," he murmured. "Maybe we ought to join him."

She flashed him a look that mingled surprise with apprehension. Then she nodded and got to her feet.

They picked their way through sprawled grown-ups and children and started down the beach. The sound of music and voices faded. Darkness closed, and Tory hugged her borrowed jacket tight. The muted, incessant rumble of the waves accompanied the rustle of the sea oats.

"I thought you didn't want to do this."

He shrugged, then realized she couldn't see the gesture in the dark. "I made you a promise. Guess I got a little derailed there for a moment, but I plan to keep it."

They took a few more steps before Tory spoke. "Do you think he'll speak to us? He didn't look especially welcoming."

He heard the tension under her question. "I think he will. Looked to me as if Gran had a few words with him. You're never too old for a talking-to from Gran."

He caught her hand in what was meant to be a reassuring gesture. Her long fingers curled around his, and his skin tingled.

How long had it been since he'd held a woman's hand while they walked? Too long, certainly. He hadn't had either the time or the inclination for dating since Lila left.

He shouldn't let Tory get her hopes up. "The thing is, if Clayton had any answers, he'd have spoken up long ago." He grimaced, knowing the darkness protected his expression. "He wouldn't keep something like that secret to protect my father. Guess you've already figured that part out."

She'd probably also guessed how Adam felt about it. He sensed her searching gaze.

"I understand they don't get along. You never did tell me just what went wrong between them."

It wasn't any of her business, was it? And yet their histories were so entangled it made little sense to try and keep it from her.

"My father uses words like lazy and shiftless to

describe his brother," he said, his voice dry. "And Uncle Clayton's been known to say that my father would sell his honor for success. You might say their values are polar opposites."

Tory was silent for a long moment. "You'd think there must be something more personal that started it."

She meant the dolphin, of course. In spite of what he knew, he wasn't quite ready to admit that. "The way I understand it, they always fought, like brothers do. But now…" Now the breach seemed wider than ever. "Maybe we'd better concentrate on hearing his version."

The string of lights that outlined the dock sent an amber glow over his uncle. Clayton sat with his back to a post, his bad leg stretched stiffly in front of him. His pipe made an orange spark in the darkness as he puffed on it.

"Kind of thought y'all would be along." He took the pipe out of his mouth and cradled it in one hand. "Seems like Tory would want to see me."

"You know who I am." Tension radiated from Tory, passing to Adam as if they were connected.

Clayton nodded. "The whole family knows. Pull up some dock and sit. I'm not sure I can help, but I'll try."

Tory sank to a cross-legged position opposite him, and Adam sat next to her. He didn't have a good feeling about this. He couldn't stop it.

"You don't favor your mother much."

Tory's hands clasped each other tightly. Was she

tired of being compared to her beautiful mother or was there more going on?

"No." Her voice had tightened. "I look like my father."

The incoming tide shushed softly against the weathered wooden boards of the dock, and the breeze lifted Tory's hair. The silence stretched. Probably neither of them knew where to start.

Adam leaned forward, planting his palms against the warm, rough planks. Looked as if it was up to him, like it or not. "My father already told us everything he knows about that night. Tory was hoping you might remember something else."

Clayton frowned absently at his pipe, then glanced at Adam with an expression he couldn't interpret. "He told you everything?"

Adam nodded. They all knew what his father had done.

"Well, I don't have much else to add, but I'll try. There were a bunch of folks there on Angel Isle that night. We'd had a crab boil." He jerked his head toward the fire that shone on the beach. "Sort of like tonight, 'cept it was all kids, mostly islanders, a few summer folk."

"Did you see my father when he came? Did you know he had the dolphin with him?" Adam found it harder to say the words than he'd expected.

"Not then. I didn't learn that until the next day, when they found out it was gone. Then I knew."

"You didn't tell." Tory's voice was soft.

"He's my brother." Clayton didn't seem to think it required more explanation than that.

"But did you see him?" Adam frowned, trying to picture what it had been like. "Was it dark when he got there?"

"Just dusk. I saw his boat come in, but I was busy with the fire. Emily was in the house, fixing something in the kitchen. Guess he went in to see her."

His hands pressed down so hard he felt as if he could launch himself off the dock. "Did you see him leave?"

"Nope, just noticed later his boat wasn't there. Emily never said anything about what passed between them, and I never spotted the dolphin that night."

"It must have been there."

Clayton shrugged. "Maybe so, but after Emily's father heard what Jefferson had to say, he and a bunch of his yacht club friends came storming in like the marines landing."

Adam was concentrating so hard on the sequence of events he almost missed it. Then he looked at his uncle, and dread hardened into a ball in his stomach. "My father told? That's how they found out?"

Clayton looked stricken. "Son, I thought you knew. You said he told you everything about that night."

"I guess he left that part out." He wanted to say his father couldn't have done that, but he knew it wasn't true. He could have. If Emily had turned him down, had scorned him for taking the dolphin, Jefferson might very well have done that.

His father had betrayed his own brother. Pain tightened around Adam's heart.

Tory made a small, distressed sound and reached toward him in sympathy. He pushed her hand away with a quick gesture. He didn't want her sympathy. He didn't want anything except to forget what he'd just learned.

But he couldn't. He had to find out everything. He swallowed hard. "Didn't Emily explain what happened with the dolphin?"

He could feel Clayton's reluctance. He shook his head slowly.

"But why?" Tory's voice sounded choked. "Surely she'd tell you what happened."

The lines in Clayton's weather-beaten face looked carved in stone. "Guess she never had the chance. I was outside, y'see, and I climbed on the lumber we had piled up for the addition to the cottage. Had this dumb idea I was going to get everyone's attention, try to calm them down."

Adam pictured a young version of his uncle clambering up, waving his arms, trying to take charge of an out-of-control situation. Something bad was coming, he could feel it.

"What happened?"

"I saw her daddy pulling Emily along. She was crying. I tried to jump down and get to her, but the wood shifted. Whole thing collapsed, came down right on top of me."

The sick taste of dread filled Adam's mouth. "You were hurt."

Clayton rubbed his bad leg. "Felt this snap—turned out it was broke in a couple of places. I heard Emily screaming as her daddy dragged her away." He shook his head. "Reckon I passed out then."

Tory rocked back and forth, hugging herself as if she couldn't stand that last image of her mother. Adam didn't know how he was going to get the picture out of his mind. Or how he'd forget his father was responsible.

His instincts had been right. The past was better off buried. Tory's determination to uncover it would lead to a lot of heartache for all of them.

Chapter Nine

"**A**re you sure you want to do this?" Tory stood on the dock late the next afternoon, watching as Adam pulled the covers off the boat's seats. He didn't look happy to be taking her to see Angel Isle, the site of the dolphin's disappearance. And after the shock they'd received the night before, she could hardly blame him.

"It's no trouble."

Adam's words were his usual response to helping someone. She'd heard him say that a dozen times since she'd been in Caldwell Cove. No trouble, he'd say with that boyish smile, regardless of the request.

Unfortunately taking her to Angel Isle was a problem for him, and they both knew it.

Clayton's revelation had blown up in their faces. She suspected Adam still hadn't come to terms with the idea that his father had not only taken the dolphin, he'd also informed on his brother.

Jefferson couldn't have foreseen the results of that angry act. It wasn't his fault that Clayton had climbed on that woodpile, but still, in some way, he must feel responsible. Clayton had to deal with a lifelong disability, and as for Tory's mother—she winced at the image of young Emily, screaming, being dragged away after seeing the boy she loved lying hurt, probably fearing he was dead.

It was small wonder Emily had never been able to forget. They all still felt the repercussions of that night, fair or not.

She leaned against the dock railing, looking at the water and letting the sun dazzle her eyes, making a reasonable excuse for any unwanted tears.

That night had changed her mother's life. She tried to shrug the tightness out of her shoulders at the thought of Emily, dragged from her summer romance, feeling guilty over what happened with the dolphin, grieving the loss of Clayton.

Was that the seed that had sprouted into drinking and depression? Or would something else have precipitated her mother's problems if that hadn't? Tory would never know.

Adam pressed the lever that lowered the boat into the water, and Tory tried to let the whir of the motor drown out all the voices in her head. The boat settled gently, rocking with the tide, and he shut the motor off. The screech of a laughing gull broke the momentary silence, and she realized she had to try again.

"Adam, I'm sure you have other things you need

to do. I can get someone else to run me out to Angel Isle. Or we can go another time.''

His brows lowered in annoyance. ''If you're going, I'm taking you,'' he said shortly. ''Hop in.''

That seemed to be that. She stepped onto the catamaran's seat, then the deck, trying to keep her stomach from misbehaving at the rocking movement. She hadn't been on a boat since her childhood, and she didn't want to disgrace herself in front of Adam. Although it hardly seemed likely he could regard her as more of a nuisance than he already did.

''Daddy, Daddy!'' Jenny's voice, accompanied by the sound of running feet, stopped his hand as he reached toward the starter. The child raced toward them along the tabby path from the house, Miz Becky behind her. ''Stop. I want to go.''

Adam leaned on the windscreen, watching his daughter as she reached the dock. ''Jenny, I've already told you that you can't go this time. Ms. Tory and I have work to do.''

Jenny grabbed the dock railing, teetering as if about to jump into the boat. ''Dad-dy!'' It was a plaintive wail. ''Take me.''

''Jenny.'' His tone was a gentle warning. ''We've had this conversation before.''

Her bottom lip came out. ''I don't want you to go with Miz Tory. You went with her last night.''

He frowned. ''What are you talking about? We all went to the picnic.''

Jenny's lips trembled. ''You went for a walk with

her all by yourselves. And my mama was lots prettier than she is.''

The child's words seemed to hit Tory right in the heart. Surely Jenny didn't think...

She backed away from the rest of that thought. Her cheeks had to be scarlet, and all she wanted to do was climb right out of that boat and disappear.

But Adam pinned her in place with a single glance. He swung onto the dock, and the power of his push set the boat rocking. He squatted to bring his face level with his daughter's.

''Jenny, there is never a good reason to make a guest in our house feel uncomfortable. I'm embarrassed by your behavior.''

His voice was firm, sounding a note of regret and disappointment. He took both the child's hands in his, the touch loving.

''I know my girl doesn't like to behave that way, does she?''

''No, Daddy.'' Jenny's voice dropped to a whisper. ''I'm sorry.''

He put his arm around her. ''It's Miz Tory who deserves your apology, sugar.''

Jenny looked at her, blinking back tears. ''I'm sorry, Miz Tory.''

She wanted to protest, wanted to explain that Jenny was wrong, that her daddy wasn't interested in Tory in any way that required a comparison with the child's mother. But she couldn't.

''It's all right, Jenny,'' she said softly, and blinked back a tear.

Adam nodded toward Miz Becky, who waited at the end of the dock. "Go on back to the house with Miz Becky, now. We'll go out in the boat together another day."

Jenny threw her arms around his neck in a throttling hug. Then she ran to the waiting housekeeper.

So that was what a father was like. Tory turned away so Adam couldn't see her tears as he dropped into the boat. That was how a real father handled his child when she disappointed him—with love, with fairness, without blame. A sudden longing for something she'd never had filled her, so intense it almost made her gasp.

By the time she'd gained control of her emotions, Adam had started the motor and begun easing the boat away from the dock.

"Adam—"

He shook his head. "Leave it, Tory."

She had no choice but to obey as he turned the boat seaward. His hands were tight on the wheel as he eased through the no-wake zone near the docks. Once clear of the area, he accelerated.

The speed pressed Tory back on the bench, and the motor's roar drowned anything she might have found to say. Adam was taking his frustration and embarrassment out in typical male fashion—speed and noise.

She settled a little more comfortably on the bench seat. She might as well enjoy the ride. Adam probably wouldn't slow down until he'd gotten the emotions out of his system.

The boat rocketed around the curve of the island,

passing the long, low yacht club with its cluster of white boats at the dock. Her gaze traced the steps she'd gone up with such anticipation the night she'd met Adam. There'd been nothing but dread filling her when she'd run down them hours later.

She shook her head, lifting her face to the wind that whipped her hair into tangles. Let the ocean breeze blow the ugly thoughts away. She couldn't go back and change the past. She could only try to make amends by fulfilling her promise.

The boat bounced over waves as Adam took the turn into the sound between Caldwell Island and the fringe of barrier islands that protected it from the open ocean. He eased back on the throttle. The roar of the motor softened to a purr, and Tory's stomach seemed to catch up with the rest of her.

"Dolphin Sound," he said, and he pointed to the waves. "And there are the dolphins it's named for."

She leaned forward, seeing nothing but the shimmer of sun on water at first. Then a silver shape lunged into the sunlight only feet from the boat. The dolphin balanced on its tail, seeming to smile at her. "He's beautiful." She grabbed her sketch pad.

"Yes." He let the boat rock gently. The dolphin slipped beneath the waves, then surfaced farther away. "I never tire of watching them."

"You couldn't." The graceful shape, water sheeting from its back, formed under her pencil. "I can't do it justice."

Adam left the wheel, coming to look at the sketch. He braced one hand on the seat back behind her, his arm brushing her shoulder and sending waves of warmth through her. He was wearing shorts and a T-shirt, and his tanned strength stole her breath.

"I think you've captured the essence, the way you did with Jenny on the swing. You're very talented, Tory."

She shook her head, reminded of the wooden dolphin and all it meant. Had its carver been satisfied he'd captured that grace and power in his work? He must have been, if he'd been willing to give his creation to the church.

She glanced at Adam, wanting to say something about the dolphin carving. He was frowning at the sketch pad.

"What is it? Did I get it wrong?"

"You got it right." He shook his head. "I was thinking about Jenny. I'm sorry about the way she behaved. She obviously thought..."

She could understand why he didn't want to finish that sentence. "She misunderstood what was happening, that's all."

"I'll talk to her. Make her see that we don't have that kind of relationship."

And what about the night you kissed me, Adam? What did that mean?

Nothing, obviously.

"I think that would be a good idea," she said carefully. "She needs to understand the situation between us so she won't be upset when we need to spend time together."

He straightened, standing between her and the sun.

"She shouldn't be upset in any event. Just because I haven't dated in the last four years doesn't mean I won't sometime."

She wanted to say she understood how Jenny felt. Wanted to say she'd been there. But if she started talking about her reactions to her father's death and her mother's remarriage, where would it end? She might give away more of herself than she'd bargained for.

"You'll make her understand," she said finally. "You're a good father."

Adam looked at her for a long moment, his gaze probing. Then he managed a half smile. "I try."

He turned to the wheel and started toward the small island across the sound. The moment she could have opened up to him was gone.

The dolphins were gone, too. A sense of loss touched her as she watched them move toward open ocean. They seemed—she struggled to formulate the thought. Somehow the dolphins symbolized this place and these people, living off the sea, moving in tune with the tides. The carved dolphin had been a fitting symbol of God's providence for the people of the island.

The small island on the horizon grew as they approached it, changing from a smudge against the sky to a mosaic of green and gold.

"Angel Isle." Adam slowed the boat as they approached a tangle of lush green undergrowth jutting into the water. He rounded it. Beyond the junglelike growth stretched a crescent of sandy beach backed by loblolly pines, live oaks and crepe myrtle, untouched and unspoiled.

Tory's breath caught at the sight. "It looks like Eden."

He cast her an approving glance. "I've always thought so." He cut the motor, and the catamaran bumped gently against a mossy dock. "Angel Isle has belonged to the family for generations."

"You're lucky."

"We are." Some emotion shadowed his face briefly. Was he thinking that Angel Isle hadn't been lucky for the Caldwell brothers one particular night? Whatever it was, he seemed to shake the feeling off as he tossed a rope around the dock's post.

"Come on." He climbed out with that deceptively easy grace and reached down to help her. "Let's have a look at the site of the infamous party."

Her determination to come here suddenly seemed as foolish as looking at the rental house. "There won't be anything to see after forty years."

"No, I suppose not." He led the way off the dock and started up a path through the undergrowth. "Still, not much has changed. You'll be able to see what it was like." He paused, nodding toward the dock. "That hasn't changed. Unless they came in something small enough to pull onto the beach, they tied up there."

She tried to visualize it. Young people—kids, really—scrambling out of their boats with towels, blankets, hampers, intent on nothing more than a good time. Probably for her mother the excursion had been even more exciting because she'd known her father wouldn't approve.

"Does your family come here often?" Did his father come back? That was what she really wanted to ask, but she couldn't quite.

Adam shrugged, and she suspected he knew what was in her mind. "In the olden days, the Caldwell clan summered here. Before air-conditioning everyone headed for the outer islands if they could."

Her father's family had summered on Tybee Island, off Savannah. Those must have been happy times, but she could barely remember.

Adam brushed a gnat away from her face. "Let's go inside before you get bitten." He led the way around a last clump of crepe myrtle. "Here's the cottage."

She stopped next to him. It wasn't a cottage at all, not that she'd expected it to be. The long, two-story building, its gray shingles merging into the gray-green background of trees and Spanish moss, stretched out a welcoming porch to them.

"I guess from what Clayton said the house was here when they had the party."

Adam nodded. "It's sat in that spot since the mid-1800s. Added onto and propped up now and then, but otherwise just the same. A summer haven for all the Caldwells. Uncle Clayton actually owns the island, but we all use it."

Her imagination peopled the porch with a young version of her mother, the golden girl, and the two boys who'd loved her.

"Your uncle said Emily was in the kitchen. If that's where she and your father talked, that must be where the dolphin was at the time."

"Let's have a look." The words sounded casual, but she could feel the tension in his hand as he touched her elbow to lead her up the steps. He unlocked the door and ushered her inside.

"You're welcome to look around the kitchen all you want." He moved away from her quickly to throw open a shutter. "But there have been a few thousand meals cooked in there, probably, since that night. You won't find anything."

A shaft of sunlight pierced the window, touching the wide plank floor, the hooked rug, the massive fireplace. Chintz-covered couches sat in front of crowded bookcases. The warm, welcoming room seemed to say that people had been happy here, despite the disturbing events of one particular night.

"Adam—" What could she say? That she had to see for herself? He must already know that.

The swinging door probably led to the kitchen. She pushed through it and found herself in a square, open room. The counters were topped with linoleum, faded from years of scrubbing. White wooden cupboards, glass-fronted, showed off a mismatched assortment of enough dishes to feed an army. Probably every time someone in the family bought something new, the old set went to the cottage.

"I'm afraid there's no place here where something could be hidden." Adam leaned against the door frame, his easy smile saying he'd gotten his momentary irritation under control.

She flipped open a bottom cupboard door at random to display neatly arranged pots and pans. The Caldwells kept a clean cottage, regardless of how much or how little time they spent here.

"I guess you're right. If it had been here, someone would have found it by now." She glanced at him, raising an eyebrow. "You're sure there are no secret passages or hidden cupboards?"

His face relaxed. "We spent some time looking for one on rainy days when we were kids, believe me. We were inspired by all those Hardy Boys and Nancy Drew mysteries on the shelves. Never found a thing."

"What's back here?" She pushed open the door on the other side of the kitchen to reveal a long room whose walls of windows seemed to invite the outdoors in.

"Game room, I guess you'd call it." Adam came to stand behind her, nodding to the table-tennis outfit and card tables. "I don't think this addition had been finished that summer, though. Maybe that's what Clayton meant when he talked about the lumber pile." Pain flickered in his eyes, and he seemed to force it away. "The kids are in and out of the closets all the time for games and toys, anyway."

"What was here before?"

"Nothing, as far as I know." He frowned. "I'm sorry, Tory. Judging from what Clayton said, most of the party must have centered outside. I'm afraid there's nothing to find here. Except—"

"Except what?"

He shrugged, still frowning. "I guess I just look at the place with different eyes after hearing about that night."

"I can see how that would be." She hesitated, wondering if she could say anything that would make him feel better about what they'd learned. "I'm sorry. About what your uncle said last night, I mean. I know it wasn't an easy thing to take."

"Easy? No." His lips tightened. "I've always known what my father's like, though. I love him, but I know he doesn't have the…" He shook his head as if he had to struggle to go on. "He doesn't have the same standards as the rest of the Caldwell clan."

"As you do," she said softly, knowing that was true. Adam was an honorable man all the way through.

He shrugged. "Funny, isn't it? My brother dealt with his feelings by rebelling. Before he left for college, our family life seemed to be one long shouting match for a while."

"You don't handle things that way."

"Nothing so dramatic for me. I was the buffer between Matt and our father. Between Dad and the rest of the family, for that matter."

She was almost afraid to breathe, afraid to disrupt the flow of his words.

"You still are, aren't you?" she said softly.

The lines around his eyes deepened. "Someone has to be."

"I guess so." Pain laced her words. "Or else the family just blows apart."

Adam put his hand lightly on her shoulder, his intent gaze focusing on her as if he looked into her heart and saw the hurt there. "That sounds like personal experience speaking."

She wanted to back away, make some excuse, change the subject. But he'd opened up to her, and that couldn't have been easy for him. She knew more about the skeletons in Adam's family closet than anyone else did. It wasn't fair to shut him out of hers.

"My father's family never approved of my mother. After his death, they wanted her to let them raise me." She tried to swallow the lump in her throat. "When she wouldn't, they washed their hands of us."

He blinked. "They must have kept in touch with you even if they didn't like Emily."

"Not a word. Not even a card on my birthday." She shrugged, trying to pass it off casually, as if it didn't still hurt. "I guess they figured losing me was a small price to pay for getting rid of her."

His grip on her shoulder tightened. "There may have been things at work you didn't understand as a child."

"You think I haven't thought of that?" The anger flared suddenly, startling her. "I wasn't a child when I graduated from high school. My grandmother came to see me. She made me an offer. They'd pay my university expenses and bring me into Savannah society. All I had to do was promise to stay away from my mother."

He didn't respond for a long moment. Was he embarrassed? She never should have said anything.

"She was stupid," he said finally.

Surprise brought her gaze up to meet his. "Why do you say that?"

He touched her cheek, the sensation featherlight but filled with a power that stole her breath away. "If she'd known anything about you, she'd have known what your response would be. She'd have known that someone who'd agree to her bargain wasn't worth anything."

"She didn't see it that way." Tory could still see her formidable grandmother, eyes cold as a glacier when she'd announced her terms. "Funny. I guess I knew even then that I wasn't going to be able to save my mother from herself. But I sure wasn't going to abandon her for the sake of that woman's money and position."

Love with strings attached, that was what her grandmother offered. There were always strings attached. She might not have known a lot about people then, but she'd known she wouldn't settle for that.

"I'm sorry." His palm flattened against her cheek, cradling it. "I shouldn't have brought it up. I didn't mean to bring back hurtful memories."

She tried to smile, but the pressure of his skin against hers seemed to have paralyzed the muscles. "We seem destined to do that to each other."

He shook his head. "We shouldn't." He barely breathed the words as he leaned closer.

He was going to kiss her. She should move, back away, say something. This wasn't a good idea. But she couldn't move. No matter how foolish it was, she wanted to be in his arms.

*   *   *

He was going to kiss her. Adam had a brief, rational instant when he knew this was a mistake. Then common sense was swamped by the need to hold her in his arms. He tilted her face up. Her eyes were dark with conflict, but she didn't pull away.

He drew her closer and covered her lips with his. Her mouth was warm and sweet and willing, and the sensation filled him with longing and need. He felt her hands slip up his back to his shoulders, holding him more fully. He was dizzy with wanting her, but he knew, bone deep, that it was more than that. He'd never felt such a need to protect, to comfort, to love.

The thought set alarm bells clanging in whatever was left of his mind. This was a mistake, a big one. He couldn't let himself think about loving any woman. He'd been there, he'd done that and he'd paid the price. And even if he could love again, it wouldn't be Tory. Too much complicated history stood between them.

He drew back slowly, reluctantly. Tory's eyes were dazed, and she braced her hands against his forearms as if he were her anchor.

He should say he was sorry, but he wasn't. Even if there could never be anything between them, he wasn't sorry he'd kissed her once.

Twice, a little voice in his brain reminded him. Three times, if you count the night you kissed Cinderella at the yacht club dance.

All right, she had an effect on him. He'd recognized that from the start, hadn't he?

Still the emotion had blindsided him as much as it had her. He brushed a strand of dark hair from her cheek. "I didn't see that coming."

She blinked, and her eyes no longer seemed dazzled. "No, I... It's all right." She tried to smile, seemed to gather her armor against rejection.

He couldn't let her think— "Tory, it's not you. I just can't get involved." He couldn't explain to her what he didn't understand himself.

"I know." Her voice was soft. "You're not ready for anyone else. You're still in love with Lila."

Her innocent words struck him like a blow. The truth beat at his brain as if demanding to be let out.

It had been one thing to let Tory believe a lie when she'd walked into his life. He'd been acting purely out of self-preservation. But now—now that he knew her, now that she'd opened up her own painful secrets to him—now it wasn't right.

"I have to tell you something," he said abruptly before he could talk himself out of it. "About my wife."

She blinked again. Whatever she'd been expecting to hear, it wasn't that. "What about her?" She took a step back and bumped into the door frame.

"You think I oppose this memorial window because of grief." He forced the words out. *You think that's why I can't let myself care for you.*

"I know." Pain darkened her eyes. "I'm sorry."

His jaw clenched. "It's not grief. I don't want a

window to memorialize a lie." The words he'd held back demanded to be said. "Lila was leaving us when she died. She was leaving Jenny and me to go with another man."

Tory stared at him, eyes wide with shock. "But everyone I've spoken with thinks—"

"Everyone thinks what I've let them think. Everyone thinks Lila and I were madly in love. Just like I did."

The harsh words tasted of bitterness. He walked away from her because he couldn't be still, ending up with his hands braced against the worn kitchen counter.

It was silent in the old house, so silent he could hear the trill of a mockingbird in the distance. Then Tory's footsteps crossed the floor behind him. Stopped.

"Why didn't you tell anyone the truth?" She sounded as if she struggled to understand. "Isn't it hard to pretend?"

"Hard? I'll tell you what would be hard." He swung to face her. "Hard would be letting my daughter know her mother was willing to give her up so she could run off with another man."

"Jenny." He heard her breath catch on the name.

"Jenny," he repeated. "She can't know that, ever. If that means I have to let all of Caldwell Cove grieve with the heartbroken widower, that's what I'll do."

Tory lifted one hand as if she wanted to touch him, comfort him. Then she let it drop. Maybe she realized how futile that effort would be. Nothing could comfort this. "Lila's mother doesn't know, does she?"

"I don't think so. If she did, I don't think she'd want to have the memorial here in Caldwell Cove."

"I'm sorry." She sounded helpless. "I understand. But what can we do about it?"

"I don't know." For the last four years he'd known what he had to do and he'd gone on putting one foot in front of the other. Now, suddenly, because of Tory, he didn't know.

"I don't know," he said again. "I just know I can't walk into church every Sunday and look at a window memorializing a lie. I can't do it, Tory."

Chapter Ten

"This hurts too much." Tory said the words aloud in the empty sanctuary. They seemed to linger under the arched wooden ceiling, almost as visible as the dust motes in a shaft of jewel-toned sunlight through the stained glass. "It's not fair."

When had love ever been fair? As soon as she thought the word, she wanted to cancel it. She didn't love Adam. And he certainly didn't have those feelings for her. He'd proved that when he'd backed away from her after those moments at the cottage on Saturday. He'd been distant ever since, even yesterday when he sat next to her for the Sunday service.

She leaned against the scaffolding, trying to get a handle on the hurt that felt as if a whale lay on her chest. She put her hand on the spot, willing it to go away. That didn't work.

On the window above her, Jesus walked across the

waves of a storm-tossed sea. From the water, Peter reached out to him in an agony of fear.

That was how she felt. Lost and afraid.

"This isn't going to work, don't You see that?" She said the words, then realized that for once in her life, her prayer wasn't filled with antagonism. "It just isn't going to work. I can't help him."

She shut her eyes. The light from the window dazzled on the blackness of her closed eyelids. If she gave up the window project—

That was what Adam wanted her to do. He hadn't asked it directly even when he'd told her the truth about Lila. But she'd known.

She opened her eyes to look at the pictured face again. The image projected calm and peace even in the midst of the storm.

"Should I give it up?" She asked the question simply, without bargaining. "Should I?"

If she did, would that help Adam? She tried to look at it without letting thoughts of her business, her success or failure, intervene. Would giving up the project help Adam?

One thing had become crystal clear that day at the cottage. Adam carried a heavy load of bitterness against his late wife. He didn't want to be reminded of those feelings every time he walked into the sanctuary that had been his place of worship all his life.

Understandable. But how could either of them get out of fulfilling this commitment?

"I just don't know what to do." That was honest, at least.

"About the new window? Or about that grandson of mine?"

The question startled Tory away from the scaffolding. She spun to face the woman who stood inside the door to the Sunday school rooms.

"Mrs. Caldwell." She had to catch her breath. "I didn't realize anyone was here."

The elderly woman came closer. "Thought you were going to call me Gran. And there's always Someone here, child. You know that."

Tory felt the wave of warmth in her cheeks. "I was talking to myself."

"You were talking to the Lord," Adam's grandmother corrected. "Nothing wrong with that. I do it myself, all the time."

It was impossible to go on feeling embarrassed when the woman looked at her with such understanding. "I'm afraid mostly I argue with Him."

"Nothing wrong with that, either. I've done my share of arguing over the years, especially over the dolphin. Is that what's troubling you?"

Tory rubbed her forehead, trying to ignore the stinging in her eyes. "I wanted to find it for my mother's sake. I thought if I could do that one last thing for her…" She trailed off. She couldn't talk about the weight she felt for Adam, for her mother's memory.

"I know." The elderly woman patted her hand. "We all have regrets, child. Things we wish we'd done differently, things we want to make up. But maybe, however much we want it, we're not meant to find the dolphin now."

"Then what good has all this been?" The question burst out. "Why did I come here?"

"We can't always know what God has in mind. Don't you lose faith in what He has for you." She gripped Tory's hand tightly, her own firm and strong. Suddenly, surprisingly, she leaned forward and kissed Tory's cheek. Without saying another word, she turned and went out.

Tory sank down in the nearest pew. *Were You speaking to me through Adam's grandmother, Lord? Were You?*

She leaned forward to grasp the pew in front of her and closed her eyes. In the stillness, she listened.

Nothing about the situation with Tory had gone as he'd expected. Adam frowned at the invoices scattered over his desk. He should be working, and instead he kept obsessing about Tory.

After baring his soul to her at the cottage on Saturday, all he'd wanted to do was withdraw. He couldn't stand seeing the pity in her eyes. He'd managed to avoid being alone with her. By Monday night, ashamed of his behavior, he'd looked for her, hoping to get things back to normal between them.

But Tory had closeted herself in the workroom immediately after dinner, making it clear she didn't want to be disturbed. Because she had work to do or because she just plain didn't want to see him? He didn't know the answer to that.

He tossed his pen onto the blotter and swiveled his chair, looking out the window at the boatyard, busy with new orders now that the summer rush of repairs had passed. Beyond the yard, October sunlight sparkled on the water. The sight reminded him that he was lucky to be doing work he loved in the place where he belonged. Today it seemed to have lost its power to soothe him.

What was he going to do about Tory?

One thing he wouldn't do was kiss her again, no matter how much he wanted to see the loneliness disappear from her eyes. No matter how much he wanted the comfort of holding her in his arms.

He wouldn't go down that road again. He'd have to handle doing without a relationship with her.

If Tory pursued the memorial window, he'd have to handle that, too. He rubbed the back of his neck, trying to erase the tension that sat there.

Maybe he'd known all along he didn't stand a chance of stopping this memorial without creating still more questions about Lila. The best he could hope for was that Tory would create some standard biblical portrayal. He could try to look at that on its own merits without thinking of Lila at all.

Yeah, right.

The door opened behind him, and he spoke without turning around. "Tina, whatever it is, can it wait?"

"It's not your secretary." The door closed. "It's me."

He spun the chair around, trying to beat down the wave of pleasure he felt every time he looked at Tory.

"Hey. What brings you here?" And how could he

gracefully tell her that maybe they shouldn't be alone together?

"I need to talk with you." She slipped the strap of her leather portfolio from her shoulder. "Do you have a few minutes?"

He made a point of glancing at his watch. "Actually, not many. Jenny's being dropped off here after school. I promised she could go out on the trial run of a new boat."

"This won't take long." Tory seemed immune to his hint. She was dressed a little more formally than usual, wearing pressed khakis instead of jeans and a scarlet sweater that made her hair look darker in contrast. He couldn't deny that he liked having her in his office even if it was a bad idea.

She propped the portfolio on the visitor's chair opposite his desk and fumbled with the catch. "I have something to show you."

Her tension leaped the few feet between them to needle him, and he guessed why she was there before she could speak. The design for the memorial window, it had to be that. His fists clenched in spite of his effort to stay detached.

Tory pulled out a large pad. "I've come up with a design."

He took a breath. Okay, he had to do this. He held out his hand. "Let me see."

She gave him the pad, then clasped both hands in front of her like a child waiting for approval. He'd just—

Tory's design swam in front of his eyes. There was

the border of beach morning glories, the space at the bottom for the inevitable inscription.

But Tory hadn't put a scriptural scene in the center. Instead, a silver dolphin leaped from a glass sea.

A vise clamped his throat, shutting off speech. The drawing was beautiful—a perfect depiction of the Caldwell dolphin. And Tory proposed putting that in a window dedicated to the woman who'd betrayed him.

He dropped the drawing as if it burned his fingers. "No." He glared at her. "No."

Her throat moved as she swallowed, but her gaze didn't falter. "I know what you're thinking. But hear me out first."

"Tory—" He shot to his feet, unable to sit still any longer. "What are you thinking? After what I told you, you ought to know I can't live with this."

"It's because of what you told me." She fired the words at him, leaning forward, her face intent and passionate. "Don't you understand? Any design I came up with would hurt you, I knew that. But if there's going to be a window, isn't it better to make it something that honors your family?"

He planted both fists on the desk. "Is this about my family or yours?"

Tory flushed as if he'd scored against her, but she stood her ground. "It's both. You told me all along we wouldn't find the dolphin. I guess you were right. There's no place left to look." She spread her hands, palms out, empty. "But this is something I can do to make up for whatever part my mother played in its loss. I thought it might make your family happy. Wouldn't it?''

"Maybe.'' Gran would be pleased, certainly. She'd have something to point to as a symbol of the Caldwell heritage. "But I'd still have to look at that inscription.'' His jaw was so tight it felt ready to shatter. "I'd still have to think about how Lila betrayed everything that heritage stands for.''

She took a step forward so only the width of the desk separated them. Her hands went out pleadingly. "Adam, think about this instead. Lila gave you Jenny. Whatever wrong she did in the end, she gave you that beautiful, perfect child to carry on your name. Doesn't that make her part of the Caldwell heritage, too?''

He wanted to say no. He wanted to forget this whole thing and return to the days before he met Tory, back to keeping his secret and carrying his burden. It had been painful, but easier.

He turned away from the drawing, rubbing his neck again. The tension had taken up permanent residence.

"I don't know,'' he said finally. "I just don't know.'' He forced himself to meet her gaze. "Can I think about this?''

"Of course.''

Running feet sounded in the outer office. "That'll be Jenny.'' He reached for the drawing, but Tory beat him to it, slipping it into the portfolio.

"It's all right.'' She gave him that rare, brilliant smile. "We'll talk about it later.''

"Thank you.'' His voice roughened on the words, and he took a deep breath, trying to regain his composure. No emotional involvement, remember? Unfortunately strong feelings, whether they were negative or positive, seemed built into every encounter he had with Tory.

A wave of relief swept over Tory. Adam hadn't rejected her idea out of hand. He'd listened to her arguments in favor of the memorial.

If only he could accept it. The idea had felt so right when she'd sat in the quiet sanctuary with his grandmother's words ringing in her ears.

Please. That would be a step toward healing for him, wouldn't it? I know creating this window would help to heal me, too.

The door burst open, and Jenny danced through, clearly excited. She saw Tory, and Tory braced herself for a repeat of the scene on the dock.

But the little girl's smile didn't falter. "Hey, Miz Tory. We're going out in the new boat my daddy made. Did you know that?"

"I heard something about it." Obviously, Adam's talk with his little daughter had borne fruit. She'd better not push her luck, though. She picked up the portfolio. "I should be getting back to work."

A look flashed between Jenny and Adam, a look of understanding without the need for words between father and daughter.

"You don't have to go yet, do you, Miz Tory? Can't you come out on the boat with us?"

The longing to do just that startled Tory with its strength. Frightened her, too, just a little. She had no future with these people, and she shouldn't create bonds that were bound to break.

"Please," Jenny wheedled. "I want you to come, honest."

"We both do." Adam's smile dissipated the lines of strain around his eyes. It went right to her heart and lodged there. "Please."

She shouldn't, should she? But Adam's asking seemed a peace offering. Besides, she wanted to.

"If you're sure I won't be in the way."

"Not at all." Adam ruffled his daughter's light brown curls. "Let's go, ladies. The *Terrapin* is ready for her maiden voyage."

"Yes!" Jenny clapped once, then raced ahead of them. They were going for a boat ride.

Walking beside Adam as they left the office, Tory tried to find some nice, neutral topic of conversation that would steer clear of anything painful.

"Jenny seems to know her way around."

He pulled the door shut behind them. "She's had the run of the boatyard since she was four. After Lila died, I wanted her with me as much as possible, so I brought her down often."

She'd managed to stumble into the wrong subject again. Still, Adam had said Lila's name with an ease she hadn't heard from him before. She'd like to interpret that as a good sign.

"So you're training the next generation to take over the family business." She fell into step with him as they went down the passageway to the docks.

He looked startled at that. "I never thought of it

that way. Whatever Jenny wants to do is fine with me. I don't believe in putting pressure on kids to be what parents want."

That struck her in the heart. "More parents should feel that way."

Adam took her arm as they walked through a tangle of tools and cables. "I feel like I'm playing it by ear most of the time."

"Then you must have perfect pitch. Jenny's a delightful child."

His eyes crinkled. "You can't say anything a father wants to hear more."

They stepped into the sunlight, and he gestured to the docks ahead of them, lining the wharf in front of a cavernous building. "We do a lot of storage and repair work here. But creating a boat from design to launch—that's the best part."

Jenny had stopped on one of the docks, chattering excitedly to an elderly man who leaned on the rail of what appeared to be— Tory blinked.

"Is that a pirate ship?"

Jenny heard the question and swung toward her, face animated. "It's our very own pirate ship, the *Jolly Roger*. This is Thomas." She gestured to the man on the deck. "He's helping us get it ready for Pirate Days. I'm going to wear a patch over my eye and sail it all the way around the island."

"The pirate ship, not the patch," Adam clarified, a note of laughter in his voice. "And I think she might have a little help with the sailing part."

Tory looked at the masts towering above them. "I'd hope so. You're really going to sail this?"

Adam grinned. "Sounds a little silly, I guess."

The gray-haired workman shook his head. "Nothin' silly about remembering." He grinned widely. "Or havin' a good excuse for a shindig after all the summer folk are gone."

"You need any help getting her ready?" Adam rested a hand on the black wooden hull. "I could spare a few hours this week."

"That'd be a help." Thomas nodded toward Tory. "We surely do want everything up to snuff if we have a guest on board."

"I'm not..."

"But Miz Tory, you have to come." Jenny grabbed her hand, jumping excitedly on one foot. "It's so much fun to play pirates."

"Give Miz Tory time to think about it," Adam said, detaching her. "Right now we've got a boat to launch, remember?"

"The *Terrapin*!" Jenny shouted, and raced down the dock.

Adam lifted a hand to Thomas as they followed. "Enthusiastic little thing, isn't she? Still, I'm pretty proud of it myself."

They passed the bulk of the pirate ship and caught up with Jenny, teetering on the edge of the dock next to a gleaming white boat. Black trim and shiny fittings completed the image of a craft fresh from the builder's hands.

Tory stopped, admiring the sleek lines. "It's beautiful. You actually built it?"

Adam climbed aboard, swung Jenny onto the deck and held out his hand to Tory. "Planed every board. Nothing mass-produced comes out of the Caldwell Boatyard. You want a custom-designed boat, that's what you get."

She took his hand, preparing to step on board, but he caught her by the waist and swung her on as he had Jenny. She stumbled, catching her breath and trying to stop the racing of her heart.

"You must be very proud of it." She hoped her voice sounded normal.

"We all are."

He nodded to the men who gathered on the dock. Two of them unfastened the lines, tossing them on board, and Jenny raced to coil them as if she'd been doing it all her life.

"Start her up, captain." Thomas grinned, and Tory couldn't mistake the look of pride and respect on his face—in fact, on all their faces.

Adam started the motor, and the *Terrapin* edged away from the dock. The men clapped, grinning. An odd shiver went down Tory's spine. Adam must feel the way she did when she'd completed a window. But he had people cheering for him, sharing his satisfaction.

She settled onto the seat behind him as he turned the new boat into the channel. "You're really an artisan, aren't you?"

Jenny wiggled onto the seat next to her. "What's an artisan?"

"Someone like me, who makes things with their hands. I make windows, and your daddy makes boats."

Jenny tipped her head to one side, considering. "I think I'd like to be an artisan, too. But I don't know what I want to make."

Adam flashed Tory an amused glance. "You have plenty of time to decide that, sugar."

They moved into the waterway, the boatyard and its buildings growing smaller behind them. Sunlight glittered on the water and turned the marshes to gold. The breeze lifted Tory's hair, the sun warmed her skin, and Jenny pressed against her arm in unconscious acceptance. The tension she'd felt since she'd walked into Adam's office slid away, like the boat slipping its moorings.

Adam glanced at her as if measuring her satisfaction. "Feels good, doesn't it?"

"I can understand why you'd never want to live anywhere else." She tipped her head back, enjoying the sunlight on her face. "It's perfect."

"Look, Miz Tory." Jenny leaned across her, pointing to a buoy in the channel. "That's an osprey's nest."

"You're quite the naturalist, aren't you?" Jenny really was an islander born and bred.

"And a sailor." Adam leaned back and reached out a long arm for his daughter. "Come on up here and help me steer her, sugar."

"Can I, Daddy?" Jenny scampered to him, and he wedged her onto the seat next to him.

"Sure you can. You're my first mate." His large hands covered his daughter's small ones on the wheel. "Keep her between the channel markers."

There was a lump in Tory's throat the size of a baseball. The relationship between Jenny and her father was a beautiful thing to see. Adam might not realize it, but if Jenny ever did find out the truth about her mother, he'd already given her enough love and acceptance to deal with it. Jenny would never doubt that she was loved unconditionally, no strings attached.

They rounded the end of the island and made the turn into the sound. Jenny wiggled around to look in her father's face.

"We should let Miz Tory have a turn. She didn't get to steer yet."

Adam dropped a kiss on her curls. "That's a nice idea, sugar."

"I can't," Tory said hurriedly, sure she didn't want the fate of what had to be an expensive boat in her hands. "I don't know how, and there's not room for both of us on that seat."

But Jenny had already slid out, and Adam stood, hand still on the wheel, freeing the seat.

"You just slip in here," he said. He gave her a reassuring smile. "Don't worry. I'll stay right behind you."

"Promise you won't let go of the wheel," she bargained, sliding reluctantly into the seat and tilting her head to see his face.

"I promise." He smiled, so close it took her breath away.

"I…I still don't think this is a good idea." Probably because she couldn't think straight with him so near.

"Sure it is." He bent down so his face was next to hers, barely an inch away. His arms brushed against hers as he held the wheel. "Look right through the windscreen as you steer. It's like driving a car."

"I don't risk beaching a car."

He tapped a gauge on the dash. "That shows you the bottom depth. As long as you keep her between the buoys, we're safe."

"And if I don't?" His nearness was doing odd things to her heart, and it took an effort to sound natural.

Adam turned to look at her, and she felt his breath warm against her cheek. "If you beach her, we'll wait for the tide to come in and float us off." His voice grew husky, as if he thought about being stranded. Together.

Her heart was beating so loudly the noise drowned everything else out. If only… The longing in her heart took form. If only she really could belong here. With him.

"I love being on the boat, don't you, Miz Tory?" Jenny sounded as if she thought she'd been out of the conversation long enough. "Isn't it just the best thing?"

"Yes." Tory's gaze tangled with Adam's, and she

couldn't see anything beyond the emotion in his eyes. "It's the best thing."

"My mommy never liked it," Jenny went on. "That's funny, isn't it?"

Adam stiffened, his hand tightening over hers so hard it hurt. But it didn't hurt as much as seeing the pleasure fade from his eyes or recognizing the truth in her heart.

Adam was still all knotted up inside over his wife's betrayal. And as long as he was, he remained tied to Lila just as surely as if she were still alive and here next to them.

Until Adam found a way to forgive the past, he'd never be free to give his heart to anyone else.

Chapter Eleven

She'd been waiting since the day before for Adam to give her his answer. She was still waiting.

Tory curled up on the overstuffed sofa in the downstairs sitting room after dinner Wednesday night. She'd discovered the small room almost by accident— it was tucked behind the formal living room. Tory found its faded chintzes and soft colors soothing in comparison to the elegance of the rest of Twin Oaks. The jewel colors of the worn Oriental carpet glowed in the lamplight.

The room didn't seem to be exuding its usual peace at the moment. She frowned at the sketch pad in her lap, reluctant to open it. She'd shown the design to Adam the day before. He'd promised to consider it and give her his answer. But the hours ticked away, and he hadn't responded. Maybe he never would.

She saw again the bleakness in his face when Jenny had innocently mentioned her mother. Adam's bitterness bound him to his late wife even more firmly than grief. How could Tory hope he'd agree to any design? How could she hope he'd be able to feel something for her?

I'm not hoping that. I'm not. But a small voice in her heart whispered that she was.

She pressed her hand against her chest as if to silence that voice. She wouldn't think about it. She'd think about the design she'd completed, about the pleasure she'd taken in choosing the glass, about the intensive labor involved in creating the life-size pattern she'd work from on the window.

All that work was worthwhile if Adam would only agree. She had to talk with him about the memorial, whether he wanted to or not.

And there was another subject on which they had to talk—one where she was the reluctant party. Should she show him? Her fingers clenched the frayed old notebook that lay under her sketch pad.

Should I, Lord? Is this the right thing to do?

She heard Adam's step in the hall, and her breath caught. "Adam?" His name was out before she thought it through.

Maybe that was for the best. God might be pushing her into this decision.

"Tory. You're so quiet I didn't realize you were back here." He lingered in the doorway, bracing one hand against the frame. He'd rolled up the sleeves of the dress shirt he'd worn at dinner, and his hair was mussed as if he'd been roughhousing with his daughter.

"Is Jenny all tucked in?"

Adam's face softened as it always did at his daughter's name. "She had to have three bedtime stories before she'd settle tonight. She's so excited about the Pirate Days celebration that she's probably dreaming about it right now."

"I know you've been busy with preparations." Is that your excuse for not getting back to me? "Do you have a couple of minutes? I'd like to talk with you."

She felt his tension from across the room. He undoubtedly thought she wanted to talk about the window, and he seemed to be searching for any excuse. And she did mean to, of course, but something else came first.

"I have some work—" It didn't sound convincing.

"This will only take a moment." The tattered notebook felt warm under her fingers, and she knew she'd made the decision. "I'd like to show you this."

He shrugged, looking harassed, then crossed the room to sit beside her on the sofa. Tory swung her feet to the floor and sat up straight, putting a few inches between them. It didn't help. She was still far too aware of his nearness.

"More sketches?" There was an edge to his words that didn't bode well for her project.

"In a way." She tried to smile and couldn't. "But not mine this time."

That caught his attention. He lifted his eyebrows. "Whose?"

She slipped the notebook from under her sketch

pad. "My mother's." She took a breath, willing herself not to let her emotions show.

"The book was your mother's?" His tone had gentled, as if he was acknowledging her grief.

"She had a couple of old trunks I had to go through after she died." She caressed the faded cover. "I found this. It's the only thing that dates from the summer she spent here."

Adam's tension was back, vibrating across the inches between them. He leaned closer. "Does she say anything about the dolphin?"

"Not in words." She opened the navy blue cover carefully, mindful of the fragile pages. "But she did this."

She handed it to him, her throat tightening as she looked at the faded drawing—the wooden dolphin on its shelf in the church, its sleek body curved almost as if in prayer.

Adam took the notebook, his hand gentle. "She did this that summer? Are you sure?"

She pointed to the bottom corner. "Yes. She dated it."

He studied the drawing. "She was a talented artist. No one ever mentions it when they talk about her."

"No, they don't." She pushed down a wave of anger. "All anyone seemed to notice was her beauty. She was much more than the way she looked."

His gaze lifted to her face as if he was assessing her emotions. "Clayton and Jefferson were teenage boys then. Teenage boys think with their hormones, I'm afraid."

"I know." She touched the page lightly. "It's only—it makes me angry that she saw herself the same way. She never tried to develop her talent or make it on her own. She let herself be defined by what other people thought." She stopped, her voice suddenly choking.

Adam's hand closed strongly over hers. "Tory, what happened to your mother wasn't your fault. You were the child, not the parent."

His words went right to the center of her pain and lodged there. How could he see so clearly what she felt? She didn't open her heart that way.

It was far better to focus elsewhere. She nodded toward the notebook. "There's another one you should see."

Adam turned the page, and his hand seemed to freeze. Lamplight cast a golden glow over the pictured faces.

Tory looked at the drawing, trying to see it through Adam's eyes. Two teenage boys, similar features, arms thrown across each other's shoulders. Jefferson's head was tipped back in laughter, and Clayton looked at his brother with a smile.

Adam cleared his throat, and his eyes were suspiciously bright. "We should show this to Dad."

Dismay flooded her. "I don't think that's a good idea. I'm sure your father feels I've interfered in your family business enough."

Adam's hand closed over hers again, warm and compelling. "Tory, this is important. He has to see this, even if it's uncomfortable."

Her gaze met his. His usual low-key, relaxed manner had been transformed into something determined and passionate that willed her agreement. She could no more resist than she could take wing and fly away.

And that was a sad comment on just how far beyond control her feelings for Adam had become.

Adam stood and held out his hand to Tory, wondering at himself. Tory was right to feel apprehensive. Interfering in the feud between his father and Uncle Clayton was playing with dynamite.

What had happened to his being the peacemaker? Peacemakers didn't set off dynamite.

Maybe he was tired of being the buffer in the family. Or maybe feeling Tory's pain over her family rift drove him. Whatever caused it, he felt compelled to do something—anything—that might make a difference.

They reached the study door. Tory hung back, her reluctance palpable. "I'm an outsider. I shouldn't be involved in this."

He didn't have to think about it. He drew her close to his side. "You're already involved. Our families were intertwined before either of us was born. Please, Tory."

She looked at him, her dark eyes huge. Then she nodded.

He tapped lightly, then opened the door. His father glanced up from the papers spread across his desk. When he saw Tory, he quickly removed the glasses he wore for reading.

"Adam. Tory. What can I do for you?" Jefferson's gaze seemed to soften as it rested on Tory, and Adam knew he was right to bring her in. Somehow, when his father looked at Tory, he saw Emily. It made him vulnerable in a way Adam had seldom seen.

"Tory has something I think you ought to see." Grasping her hand, he drew her across to the desk. He held out the notebook. "This was her mother's. From the summer she was here."

He sensed his father's withdrawal. It wasn't surprising Jefferson preferred to ignore that time in his life.

Determination stiffened in Adam. He wouldn't let his father pretend any longer.

"Look at it." His words probably came out a little more peremptory than they should, but they worked. His father took the notebook.

"I'm not sure what all the—" The sketch of the dolphin confronted him, silenced him.

Tory's fingers clenched Adam's tightly, and he gave them a reassuring squeeze. This was the right thing to do. He was sure of it.

His father didn't move for a long moment, and Adam suspected Tory held her breath just as he did. Finally Jefferson touched the page.

"I remember when she drew this." He sounded very far away. "I found her sitting on the church steps, sketching. She said she wanted to draw the dolphin. I knew where the key to the sanctuary was, so I took her inside."

They stood silent, listening.

"She was so entranced with the dolphin. I'd never seen her like that. Why should she care about something in a little church on a little island? After all, she had everything."

The words touched Adam's heart. Had that encounter been the beginning of his father's need for success at any cost? His feeling that the girl he loved had everything while he had nothing?

Adam cleared his throat. "Maybe you ought to look at the next page."

Jefferson turned the sheet over carefully. His hand froze. Nothing broke the silence but the tick of the grandfather clock.

Adam willed his father to speak, sensing that Tory felt the same. They seemed linked through their clasped hands, or maybe through something more elemental that he didn't comprehend.

At last Jefferson put the notebook on the desk. He touched the pictured faces lightly with his fingertips.

"So long ago." He shook his head. "I remember. We were so close, long ago."

"You could be again." Adam forced the words out. "You could be, if you want it enough."

His father's mouth worked as if he tried to hold back emotion. "It's too late for that. We've said too many painful things."

"It's not too late." Adam leaned forward. "It doesn't have to be. You need to make the first move."

A sudden flare of anger chased the sorrow from his father's face. "Why should I do that?"

Adam held his gaze, knowing he was about to say

something that could create a breach between them. Knowing, too, that he had to say it. "Because you were wrong. You know you were wrong."

Jefferson glared at him for a moment. Then, quite suddenly, tears welled in his eyes. He shook his head, blinking. "I know. I was wrong. But I don't know how to make up for it."

Adam could breathe again. "You can find a way if you really want it. Just take one small step toward him, that's all."

One step. He held Tory's hand, knowing he should take his own advice. He needed to take one small step that would set things right between them.

It wasn't Tory's fault his wife had betrayed him. It wasn't her fault his mother-in-law had unwittingly given her an impossible job.

He had to take one small step. The trouble was, he didn't know if he could.

Tory turned off the soldering iron and pushed her protective goggles to the top of her head. She stretched, trying to get the kinks out of her back, and looked with satisfaction at the window of Jesus walking on the water, touched by the last rays of the setting sun.

It was finished. Each piece had been painstakingly cleaned and the damaged pieces replaced. The fresh look of the new lead would quickly fade. The window was as lovely as it had been a hundred years ago. She only wished she could feel as happy with her original work.

She stretched again, then moved slowly to the workroom's other table. She'd done everything she could to prepare to work on the new window. Everything except begin.

She looked longingly at the full-size design, carefully smoothed and taped to the tabletop. Unfortunately being ready didn't do her any good. Nothing would, unless and until Adam gave his approval.

She gripped the edge of the table. She'd thought, after the way they'd opened up to each other the previous night, that it would make a difference in Adam's attitude. Apparently she'd been wrong.

Father, is this going to work at all? She touched the design longingly. *I think I could do something beautiful to Your glory, if only Adam would let me.*

She closed her eyes, trying to listen to her heart. She didn't hear an answer.

"Tory? May I come in?"

She whirled at the sound of Adam's voice. He lingered in the doorway, as if the workroom belonged to her instead of to him. With his creased chinos and white knit shirt, his hair wet from the shower, he looked ready for an evening out.

She wiped her hands on her jeans, then pushed her hair from her face. She probably looked ready to clean the trash cans.

"Of course, come in." She moved quickly to the repaired window, not sure she wanted him looking at the new window she'd laid out. He might think she'd started work on it in defiance of his wishes. "This window is ready to go back whenever your crew can take it.''

He stood next to her, looking at the window. He smelled of soap and sunshine, and his nearness sent a little shimmer of pleasure across her skin.

"You've done a wonderful job. I didn't realize how dim the window had become until you cleaned it." He touched the stained glass reverently. "This has always been my favorite."

"You have good judgment. The artistry in this one is special." She stopped, shaking her head. "The waves are so real, you can almost feel Peter's fear."

"Maybe that's why islanders love it so much. They know what the sea can do."

Was he thinking of that shipwrecked ancestor of his? Or of more recent storms?

"It was a joy to work on. I almost felt in touch with the artisan who created it." She smiled. "That's a good feeling, believe me."

"I guess it would be. Sort of like working on a good boat. You know that your labors are worthwhile."

"Exactly." She smiled at him, feeling in tune for a moment.

He touched her arm lightly, and his expression was very serious. "I've been wanting to tell you. You did a good thing last night, Tory. Thank you for showing me your mother's drawings. And thank you for going with me to my father."

"I hope—" She hesitated, not sure she should say what she was thinking. "I believe my mother saw restoring the dolphin as a means of repairing the damage caused by what happened that summer." She chose her words carefully. "I don't mean just the harm to the church, but the trouble between your father and his brother."

His jaw tightened, the movement barely perceptible, but she saw it. "She wasn't the only cause of their problems, as far as I can tell. Their quarrel over her was just the latest in a string of incidents."

"Regardless, she felt responsible. She wanted the dolphin returned, but it doesn't look as if that's going to happen." She felt her throat tighten. "There's no place left to look, we both know that."

His hand closed over her wrist, and she felt his sympathy flow through it. "Tory, I'm sorry. I wish we'd had a happier outcome."

"You tried. I appreciate that."

"It was a pleasure." His voice roughened on the words, and she looked at him, startled. His eyes had darkened, and he seemed to search for words. "I didn't expect to, but I've enjoyed the time we've spent together."

"That almost sounds like goodbye." She tried to say it lightly, but she was afraid her voice betrayed her.

"Goodbye?" Surely that was genuine surprise in his voice. "Why would I say goodbye?"

She nodded toward the stained glass. "That's the last of the repair work. If you don't want me to start on the new window, then I guess I'm done here."

"No." He shook his head irritably. "I mean, no, I

don't want you to leave. I want you to go ahead with the dolphin window.''

A spurt of joy shot through her, but it was quickly tempered by the way he'd expressed himself. Apparently Adam still couldn't refer to it as the memorial window. That fact sent warning bells clanging in her mind.

''Are you sure?''

He turned away from her and looked at the design she'd spread on the other table. She studied the rigid line of his shoulders, wishing she could ease the tension away and make him happy.

''I'm sure,'' he said finally. He tapped the table. ''You have a good design here, Tory. This window is as much for Jenny as for anyone. I want her to see the Caldwell dolphin in the church one way or another.''

He still wasn't mentioning Lila. Maybe she should say something, but she couldn't. If he intended to let her go ahead with the project, that was the best she could hope for. She'd have to be content.

''Thank you, Adam. I'm glad. I'll try not to let you down.''

He swung toward her, and she had the sense that his tension eased as soon as he wasn't looking at the design. Would he really be able to cope with the finished product?

His smile flickered. ''You won't let us down,'' he said. ''Your dolphin will be beautiful.''

''Will it make up for coming here and prying into your family's past?'' Into your past, she'd almost said, but she'd caught herself in time.

Adam leaned against the table, his long-limbed figure seeming relaxed now that he'd made the decision. "I think, in the long run, a little prying will make things better. Maybe we can put this stupid feud behind us, once and for all."

"I hope that's so." She probably wouldn't be here to see it, but she hoped he was right.

He braced his hands behind him on the table edge, careful not to touch the design. "That wasn't the only reason I came in to see you, by the way."

"Then why?"

He smiled. "You've been ignoring Pirate Days. And that's not easy to do when all of Caldwell Cove is caught up in the excitement."

"I've noticed. But I don't belong to Caldwell Cove, remember?"

He shrugged that off. "You have as much reason to be part of the celebration as anyone. Jenny and I want you to join us."

"Join you?"

"Sail on the *Jolly Roger* with us for Pirate Days. Everything starts a week from Saturday, with the regatta. There's a dinner and dance that evening, then a church service with the blessing of the boats on Sunday."

"It sounds lovely. But isn't sailing the ship just for your family?"

"Family, friends. We're inviting you, Jenny and I. We want you to be a part of the *Jolly Roger*'s crew."

"But..." A dozen objections leaped into her mind. "I don't know anything about sailing a pirate ship."

He grinned. "You don't have to. You can be the royal maiden kidnapped by the pirates."

"I don't think I brought any royal maiden dresses with me."

He brushed that aside with a quick gesture. "We have years' worth of costumes around. We'll find something for you. Come on, say you'll do it. You don't have to work all the time, you know."

"Well, I..." She couldn't believe how appealing it sounded to take part in something that made him so happy. "Are you sure Jenny wants me to come?"

"She does." He took both of her hands in his, and their warmth seemed to flow right up her arms and touch her heart. "We both do."

He didn't mean anything by it, she knew that. As long as she knew it, she'd be safe from letting him bruise her heart again.

And she'd have a lovely memory to take with her when she left Caldwell Island.

"All right. I'd love to."

Chapter Twelve

"I thought you said I got to be the royal maiden." Tory swung the paintbrush against the mast of the *Jolly Roger* and glanced at Adam, who was doing the same thing on the other side of the mast. "You didn't mention anything about being a painter's assistant."

He grinned, looking relaxed and happy in his paint-daubed jeans and T-shirt. "You were working too hard. I thought you needed a break."

"Are you saying this isn't work?" She bent to dip her brush in the can of black paint.

"At least you're using different muscles."

How would you know what muscles I use on the windows, Adam? How would you know anything about it? You haven't been in the workroom for the last week.

He hadn't done more than thrust his head into the room when he came to urge her to help with some last-minute painting to ready the pirate ship for the following day. All week, since the night he'd told her to go ahead with the window, he'd avoided the workroom as if it pained him to be near it.

Well, maybe it did. She should be glad her work was going well. She didn't have the right to expect Adam to be happy about it.

Certainly the congregation had seemed pleased with the repair work at church on Sunday. Pastor Wells had thanked her again from the pulpit, and most of the church members had stopped to add their words of appreciation after the service.

"Everyone's happy about the windows, you know." Adam seemed to be reading her mind. "I can't tell you how many people have commented about your work."

She knelt to touch up some chipped places at the base of the mast. "I enjoyed being there Sunday to hear what they thought of it. Usually when you work in a church, you're not around long enough to see people's reactions to what you did."

"Is that mostly what you do?" He looked at her, seeming genuinely interested. "Church windows?" It was the first time he'd mentioned her work other than in the context of the problem between them.

"My last employer did all sorts of projects, but he ran a big studio. I'd like to specialize in church projects—both repair work and new designs."

She half expected him to tense at the mention of new designs, but he didn't seem distressed. "Why church works, especially?"

She couldn't say this to just anyone. But she could

to him. "The other work is satisfying, but church windows give me the chance to express my faith in my designs. What is better than that?"

He nodded. "I guess I feel that way about the boatyard. We have to do repairs—that's the bread and butter. But creating our individual boats for customers who want quality craftsmanship is where the joy comes in."

"Exactly. Joy is just the right word." They were connecting at a level she hadn't expected on a subject that had to be touchy where Adam was concerned.

She sat on the sun-warmed deck, finding it easier to paint that way. Adam had been right—this did use different muscles. But at least here at the boatyard she could feel the sun beat on her back and smell the mingled aromas of salt air, fish and paint.

"So what made you start your own business? Weren't you able to do what you wanted with the last studio you worked for?"

His question made her feel she was the one being pushed into a touchy area. She could evade the truth, but Adam had been honest with her. She owed him the same. And they were alone, with every other worker out of earshot.

"I liked the work, all right." She took a breath, then forced herself to look at him. The sunlight dazzled her eyes. "The problem was, I was engaged to the firm's owner. When our relationship fell apart, I didn't fit in any longer. It seemed time to go out on my own."

Adam's brush paused in its even strokes. He squatted on his heels across from her, face intent. "What happened to your engagement?"

She wanted to resent the question but she couldn't, not when it was filled with such caring.

"I thought Jason and I were a team," she said carefully. She hadn't said this to anyone, but she was going to tell Adam. "We'd done a big project—the one I showed you in the magazine spread. I was the designer on that job, but when the project began to get some attention, Jason made it clear that he expected to receive all the credit for the designs."

The realization didn't hurt as much as it had once, but it still stung.

"I saw that wasn't the kind of relationship that would make for a good marriage."

She studied the black-and-white label on the paint can as if it fascinated her, so she wouldn't have to look at Adam. "That was when I decided to strike out on my own."

"And you ended up in Caldwell Cove." He reached out to touch her paint-stained hand. "I'm glad."

Are you, Adam? Her breath caught. Could she possibly believe he meant anything by it?

Then he stood, putting the lid on the paint can, and the moment was over. Maybe that was just as well. She shouldn't be reading anything into the kindness Adam dealt out to everyone who crossed his path. It didn't mean he had feelings for her.

"Here comes Jenny." He shaded his eyes, looking toward the road. "We're about to get some help." He smiled. "That's why I closed the paint can."

"Wise man." Keep it light, remember? That way nobody got hurt.

"Trust me, I learned my lesson the hard way. You don't want to know what happened when we painted the barn last year. It took six months for Jenny's pony to look normal again."

She stood, taking the rag he tossed her and wiping her hands. "You're right, I don't want to know." She glanced at her watch. "Isn't it too early for her to be out of school?"

"You really haven't caught on to how seriously we take Pirate Days, have you? Even school dismisses early so the children can help get ready. They consider it an educational event."

He seemed to be serious.

"You're not telling there were actual, historical pirates, are you? I thought this was just an excuse to have a little fun."

"Hey, Daddy. Hey, Miz Tory. What can I do?" Jenny skidded to a stop perilously close to the paint can.

Adam grabbed her. "Hey, yourself. Take it easy. You just got your cast off, remember? You don't need another one."

"I'm always careful, Daddy." Jenny didn't look especially impressed with the warning. "What can I do? Can I paint?" She reached eagerly toward a wet brush, and Adam caught her hand.

"You can tell Miz Tory about the pirates. She doesn't think they were real."

"Not real?" Jenny's eyes widened. "We learned all

about them in school, Miz Tory. It's real, honest. The pirates used to hide around the sea islands. Some people even say they buried treasure here. Why, one time somebody even found a gold Spanish coin in an old log.''

Tory looked from Jenny to Adam. Both of them certainly seemed to be taking it seriously. ''So this parade with the boats tomorrow—''

''It's to remember when a pirate named John Law took over the island in 1802.'' Jenny rattled the facts off as if she'd memorized them. ''His ship was called the *Jolly Roger,* and ours is meant to look just like his.''

''Very good.'' Adam ruffled her hair, then smiled at Tory. ''We do have a few modern innovations, though. The pirates storm ashore at the yacht club, for instance, which obviously wasn't there in 1802. And nobody really walks the plank.''

''I'm relieved to hear it.''

''I have a costume like Daddy's, Miz Tory. Did you get your costume yet?''

She glanced at Adam. ''Actually, I forgot all about it. Was I supposed to look for one?''

''Nope. It's all taken care of.'' He caught Jenny's hands and swung them back and forth, making her giggle. ''Miz Tory is going to look like a princess.''

''I get to be a pirate,'' Jenny declared. ''With an eye patch and everything. That's better. But you'll make a nice princess, Miz Tory,'' she added generously.

Tory felt a slight tremor of apprehension. What exactly was this costume? "I've never considered myself the princess type."

"Oh, I don't know." Adam's face crinkled with amusement. "I seem to remember a time when you were Cinderella."

"That was a long time ago," she said firmly. "I'm a craftsman now, not a princess."

She realized suddenly that they were talking easily, even joking about the night that had haunted her for such a long time. She wouldn't have thought that possible before she'd come back to Caldwell Cove.

Maybe she and Adam were moving toward accepting the past. If so, this trip had been worthwhile even without finding the dolphin.

Jenny grabbed her hand. "Miz Tory, can I come see the window you're making for my mommy? Miz Becky keeps saying I have to wait, but I want to see it now."

Jenny's sudden change of subject caught her off guard. "If it's okay with your daddy."

"No." The word came out with explosive force. She looked at Adam to find his eyes suddenly as gray and bleak as a storm on the ocean. "It's not okay."

Her heart stuttered. She'd been wrong. The knowledge was a physical pain that cut through her. Adam wasn't accepting the past at all.

Now where had that come from? Adam shook his head, hoping he could shake off the feelings that had erupted with Jenny's innocent question. His response had been instinctive, but it hadn't been fair to either Jenny or Tory.

"Sorry, sugar." He touched his daughter's cheek lightly. "I didn't mean to sound like a bear."

Jenny pouted. "Well, you did. A growly bear. I don't see why I can't look at the window."

"Nobody's looking at it until it's finished." That was the first reasonable excuse for his behavior that popped into his head, and he could only hope it sounded good to both of them. "I'm sure Miz Tory will be finished with the window soon, and then you can see it before anybody else, okay?"

"It'll be ready in just a couple more days," Tory said quickly. "I'll tell you when."

"Okay." Jenny's smile reappeared. "Now can I help paint?"

The tension inside him eased. "We're finished with the painting, but Uncle Matt's about ready to swab the deck. How about helping him?"

"I can do that." Jenny whirled and darted toward the stern. "Uncle Matt, I can help you," she called.

Jenny was easily distracted, and just as easily forgiving. Tory was something else again. He turned to her, trying to find an excuse for his behavior. There wasn't one.

"I'm sorry." He spread his hands, palms up. "That was stupid."

Her mouth was tight. He might have thought it expressed anger, but he could see the hurt hiding in her eyes.

"You have a right to do what you want." She

turned away. "But she'll have to see the window sometime."

"I know. Tory..." His voice trailed off. What else could he say?

His gaze traced the pale skin of her nape, the tension in her shoulders, the curve of her back. Vulnerable. He'd seen it that first day when he'd looked into Tory's dark eyes and recognized loneliness.

Tory put on a good front of being determined and independent and depending on nobody. But he knew better. He knew just how tender she was inside.

She wasn't the only one. He tried to look honestly at his feelings. He was drawn to Tory in a way he'd never been drawn to another woman, even Lila. Lila had been youthful infatuation masquerading as reality. Tory was real. Tory had somehow reached him through all the defenses he'd erected after Lila's betrayal.

But they were both too wounded to love again. That was the bottom line. He had to be careful.

"I'm sorry," he said again finally. "I want Jenny to see the window. I know she'll be happy with it."

And I'm sorry I hurt you, Tory. That was what he felt, but he didn't think he could say that. At least not out loud.

Tory stood before the oval mahogany mirror in her bedroom the next day, mentally ticking off all the ways she didn't resemble any princess she'd ever heard of.

Princesses didn't wear faded sweat suits and sneak-

ers. They didn't have a tangle of dark hair. They didn't
look ready to scrub the floor. Cinderella, even before
the fairy godmother dusted her off, had undoubtedly
been a blond-haired, blue-eyed beauty.

Like her mother.

She pressed her fist against her midsection. She
might as well tell the truth, at least to herself. This
sudden panic wasn't over whether she did or didn't
resemble a princess. She was afraid because she didn't
belong.

Adam Caldwell, with his flock of relatives and his
self-assured, confident air, couldn't possibly understand that. He'd always known he belonged here.
She'd never belonged anywhere.

A rap on the door interrupted the morbid turn her
thoughts had suddenly taken. Straighten up, she told
herself sternly. *You can pretend you're part of this, at
least for one day.*

She opened the door. Miz Becky stood there, her
arms filled with a frothy confection in emerald green.

"Time's a-wasting, child." She bustled into the
room, spread the gown on the bed and looked at it
with satisfaction. "We got to get you ready."

"That's for me?" Tory felt a wave of light-
headedness. "I didn't expect anything like that. Adam
just said there were some old costumes around."

"He must have been joking. He rented this gown
special from the costume shop in Savannah where they
got the pirate outfits." She stroked the silk once, then
crossed to the dressing table and picked up a brush.
"Come on, now. Let's get your hair fixed first."

Tory's hands flew to her unruly mop. "I don't expect you to do my hair. I'm sure you have lots to do getting ready yourself."

Miz Becky's eyes crinkled in amusement. "Nobody's getting me on a pirate ship, I can tell you that. So I got plenty of time to dress for the party. Right now, all I want is to see you turn into a princess. Come on now. Don't be giving me any excuses."

Tory took a seat reluctantly at the dressing table, and Miz Becky began brushing her hair from her face. "I still don't think—"

"Don't think, then. Just enjoy." She swept Tory's mane up, pinning it into place with clips she took from her apron pocket. "I tell you the truth, it does my heart good to see Adam so excited about this day. He hasn't been this pleased about the celebration since I don't remember when."

Tory's gaze caught Miz Becky's in the mirror. "Really?"

The housekeeper nodded. "Honest." She picked up the curling iron and began taming Tory's curls. "Ever since Lila left, he's been going through the motions. It's good for him to be looking forward to this day. He's been unhappy about that for too long. It's time he got over it. Time he moved on with his life."

"I'm not sure he can move on when he's still grieving," Tory said cautiously.

"I don't reckon it's grieving he's been doing all this time."

Apparently Miz Becky did know. Did Adam realize

someone who knew him as well as Miz Becky did had guessed?

"Maybe not grieving," she conceded. "But he's—" She bit her lip. She shouldn't be talking about him this way. But Miz Becky loved him. "He's still bitter."

The woman nodded, as if Tory had given the right answer. "That woman's got him tied to her by that. It's high time he got free."

She didn't seem to expect an answer, just concentrated on putting the finishing touches to Tory's hair. Tory hardly noticed, she was so busy wrestling with Miz Becky's words.

She was right. Adam's bitterness tied him to the memory of Lila's betrayal. He hadn't forgiven her. That was why he couldn't look at the window in her memory. Not because it reminded him of her, but because it reminded him of his inability to forgive.

Is that it, Lord? Is that why Adam has been confronted with this window—because he has to forgive?

"Now you just stand still and let me put the dress on you." Miz Becky's deft fingers adjusted the layers of petticoats.

She lifted the dress, and Tory felt the whisper of silk as it fell into place. Miz Becky fastened it, then twitched the skirt until it hung to her satisfaction.

"There," she said, turning Tory toward the mirror. "Now look."

Tory blinked. The elegant stranger looking back at her certainly wasn't plain, workaday Tory Marlowe. "Is that really me?"

Miz Becky threw back her head and laughed. "Sure is. You do look like a princess today." She pressed her warm cheek briefly against Tory's. "You go down there and do us proud. Adam's waiting for you."

Adam. Her heart skipped a beat. What would Adam think of this?

She let herself be hustled out of the bedroom to the stairs. She stopped at the top of the sweeping stairway for a moment, clutching the polished rail. It wouldn't do a thing for the elegant getup if she tumbled all the way down, would it?

"Keep your head up and hold your skirt with one hand," Miz Becky advised. "How women ever did anything at all in an outfit like that is beyond me, but you surely do look beautiful."

She wanted to reject the words. She hadn't been beautiful a day in her life. But maybe she could pretend, just for today.

That thought gave her the courage to lift her chin, grasp her skirt and walk slowly down the stairs. As she came around the curve of the stairway, she saw Adam waiting at the bottom. He watched her with open admiration, and her heart skipped again.

No man had any right to look like that. Adam's boy-next-door good looks had been transformed by the black pants, high boots and white buccaneer shirt. A black eye patch gave him an unexpectedly dangerous look.

She reached the hallway without incident. Adam took her hand, swept her a bow.

"You look wonderful." He lifted her hand, and the

brush of his lips on her skin sent shivers racing up her arm. "Wonderful."

Jenny, wearing an identical pirate outfit, ran to her. She pirouetted. "I'm a pirate, too, just like Daddy."

"You're a very convincing pirate," Tory said.

"You look like a princess, Miz Tory." Jenny grabbed her hand.

"She looks like Cinderella."

"But Daddy, Cinderella should have glass slippers." Jenny seemed prepared to argue the point.

"Cinderella," Adam said firmly, tucking Tory's hand into the crook of his elbow, "Shall we go?"

It's pretend, she told herself desperately. Just pretend. We're all pretending.

It didn't feel like pretence to have her hand clasping Adam's strong arm. Or to have Jenny clinging to her other hand. It felt like belonging. And that was a dangerous thing to start believing.

Chapter Thirteen

It wouldn't be hard to convince herself she'd fallen into a fairy tale, Tory thought as she leaned back in her deck chair. White sails billowed in the breeze, and the pirate pennant above her head snapped. The *Jolly Roger* moved into the channel to the accompaniment of seagulls squawking and bells clanging.

Adam stood at the wheel with Jenny in front of him, his strong hands covering her small ones. His gaze found Tory's across a deck crowded with Caldwells and their friends, and he gave her a smile of such pure pleasure her breath caught. He should look that carefree and happy always.

"Reckon Adam likes being a swashbuckler for a day." Adam's grandmother, seated next to Tory, watched him with approval in her sharp eyes. "It's good for that boy to cut loose once in a while."

"He doesn't cut loose often, does he?"

"Land, no." Mrs. Caldwell shook her head.

"Maybe that's how he wants it." Adam's loyalty to his family, even to his late wife—well, it was admirable, wasn't it?

The elderly woman regarded her, and Tory felt as if her heart and soul were being carefully examined. "I s'pose he does. Guess you'd know that, since you're one of the responsible ones, too."

"Me?" The idea startled her. "I'm on my own. Responsible to no one."

Adam's grandmother shook her head. "You can't deny your nature, child. No one can. You came here because you felt responsible, though you weren't even born when the dolphin disappeared."

She hadn't thought of it that way. She'd only known that recovering the dolphin was one thing she could do for her mother.

"Responsible or not, I didn't succeed." Her throat tightened. She'd failed to fulfill that last promise. "I didn't find it."

Mrs. Caldwell smoothed the gray lace of her dress. "I'd like to see that dolphin back where it belongs, too, but you know things happen in God's own time, not ours."

"Gran, you're not harping on that dolphin again, are you?" Miranda Caldwell settled into the chair on the other side of Tory. With her bronze hair and her Civil War era dress and hat, she reminded Tory of Scarlett O'Hara. "I know you miss it, but we're doing all right even without the dolphin there for weddings."

"I don't see you settling down to happily-ever-after,

young lady." Her grandmother's voice was tart. "Seems like you need to find somebody to love."

Miranda snapped open a lace fan, and it hid her face for a moment. "Could be that's not meant to happen, Gran. Dolphin or no dolphin." The smile she gave Tory seemed strained. "You have to forgive Gran. She's got this notion that Caldwells are supposed to be married under the dolphin."

"It's not a notion." Her grandmother leaned forward in the chair as if she'd jump up and set things right if she could. "There's a lot more truth in legends and such than you young folk want to believe."

"All right, Gran," Miranda said hastily. "I believe you."

"That dolphin belongs in the church, and things won't really be the way they're supposed to be till then." She looked from Miranda to Tory. "And that's the truth."

Tory clenched her fists against the green silk. "I wish I'd been able to make that happen." She looked at Adam again, her gaze tracing the lines of his strong face. A good face, one meant for more happiness than he'd found. "For all of you."

Mrs. Caldwell reached over to clasp her hand in a firm grip. "Don't you blame yourself, now. It's all in the good Lord's hands. We just have to trust it will work out the way He plans. Besides, maybe you're here for another reason altogether."

Tory's heart seemed to stutter. "I don't know what you mean." What did those wise old eyes see in her?

Miranda had turned away to say something to her

young son, and Adam's grandmother leaned closer, her words just for Tory. "Seems to me maybe you and your window can help Adam put the past behind him."

For a moment she couldn't speak. But such honesty seemed to demand honesty in return. "I haven't done such a good job of ignoring the past in my own life."

Gran patted her hand. "Not ignore, child. Forgive. If you've got a ways to go, maybe you'll help each other. Nothing wrong with that."

"I don't think—"

"Don't think so much." Gran's wise old eyes twinkled. "That's the trouble with you young ones, you think too much. Just let your heart guide you."

Tory let the words sink in, her gaze on Adam. If she listened to her heart right now, what was it telling her? Maybe it was saying to relax and enjoy this day without worrying so much about tomorrow.

Adam looked at her and smiled again, and her heart fluttered. He couldn't possibly have heard what they'd said, but he seemed to be communicating directly with her. He held out his hand.

"Come along and help me steer this thing, Tory," he called.

She could almost feel Adam's grandmother pushing her out of the chair. She crossed the deck, mindful of the unaccustomed long skirt, and joined him.

Adam had shoved the eye patch back, but he still had a devastatingly dangerous look in that pirate outfit. She had to clamp down on a rush of longing.

"I don't think you really want my help," she said. "I don't know a thing about boats, remember?"

"Just stand here and talk to me, then." He gave a quick, experienced glance at the sails, then turned his smiling gaze on her. "My first mate deserted me to play with her cousins."

Tory looked at the crowd lining the rails and sitting on the deck. Jenny had linked arms with her cousin Andi and seemed to be attempting a jig. "Looks like quite a group of Caldwells."

He nodded. "The family always sails the *Jolly Roger*, and we take turns being the captain. This is my lucky year." He gave Tory a look that might mean, if she really let herself imagine things, that meeting her again was part of that luck.

She suspected her cheeks were red. "Seems as if the whole island gets in on the act."

"You bet." He nodded toward the clutch of small boats that bobbed along in the ship's wake, escorting the *Jolly Roger*. "Watch what happens. Each time we pass a dock on our way around the island, we'll pick up more boats. By the time we reach the yacht club, half the islanders will be with us, and the other half will be waiting there."

"So there is something the islanders and the yacht club crowd do together."

He frowned briefly, then shrugged. "I guess you're right. I hadn't thought about it, but this is the one time of the year that all the barriers come down."

It would be nice to believe those weren't the only barriers that could fall. But what kept her from Adam was far more elemental than the money and tradition that separated the islanders from the summer people. She ought to remember that.

It wasn't easy when Adam caught her arm and drew her closer. "Put your hands here on the wheel and feel how she responds."

The *Jolly Roger* wasn't the only female who responded. With Adam's hands covering hers, his breath warm on her neck, her heart swelled.

"Like this?" The polished wheel felt smooth beneath her fingers, and Adam's grip was firm and sure. "I don't want to run us aground."

"You won't." His breath caressed her cheek. "I'll take care of you."

Something that might have been hope blossomed inside Tory. Maybe it was time to stop telling herself this couldn't work—and to follow her heart.

Adam didn't want to let her go. Glancing at Tory, next to him as she had been for most of the trip, Adam knew he was in trouble. This woman had taken possession of his thoughts and feelings, maybe of his heart.

That jolted him right down to his soles. He couldn't let himself feel this way. He couldn't give his heart to another woman.

Tory isn't Lila, a small voice whispered in his mind. *Tory is honest, forthright, caring. She wouldn't trample on your love.*

He frowned, automatically checking the sails as he made the last sweeping turn around the curve of the island. Was that really what he was doing—letting Lila's betrayal sour him on any other woman?

The yacht club, its dock crowded with people, came into view. His gaze traced the wide white steps. He'd hurried down those steps looking for Tory that night, when he'd realized she wasn't coming back. But all he'd found was the white rose she'd worn in her hair, lying forgotten on the walk.

What would have happened if Tory hadn't disappeared that night? His heart clenched. How different would their lives have been?

He couldn't let himself think that way. No matter how much Lila had hurt him in the end, she'd given him Jenny. His daughter was worth any price. Even if he could go back and change things, knowing what he knew now about how they'd end up, he wouldn't.

Not change the past, no. But what about the present? What about seizing the present?

The swashbuckler he was portraying would do that, but Adam was pretending. A costume didn't turn him into a different person.

"I didn't realize there were that many people on the island." Tory's voice interrupted his thoughts before he could argue that he was really a swashbuckler at heart. "There's quite a crowd to greet you."

Adam glanced at his crew, making sure they were all at their stations. "The whole island's watching us bring the *Jolly Roger* in. It's not a time when you want to miss the dock. Or worse, crash into it."

Tory took a step back as if to give him more space.

"I'm not worried." Her voice was filled with confidence. "You'll do it."

He could only hope her trust wasn't misplaced. He gauged the current, the wind and the rapidly narrowing space between the prow and the dock. He called out his orders, knowing he could trust his brother and cousins to move quickly.

The *Jolly Roger* seemed to curtsey on the waves. There was a moment of tension when he wondered if he'd judged it right. Then the prow kissed the dock as smoothly as if he did this every day of the week.

He heard the cheers and clapping, but they were background music. All he could think about was the delighted expression on Tory's face when he turned to look at her.

"That was wonderful."

"Not bad," he said.

She leaned closer, and he caught the faint scent of roses that seemed to surround her. It reminded him of playing in the shade of his grandmother's flower beds on a warm afternoon.

"What happens next?"

He nodded toward the crew as they swarmed ashore. "Our pirates are going to take control and raise the Jolly Roger flag. Then we all adjourn to the yacht club for dining and dancing."

She smiled. "Undoubtedly what the original pirates did."

"Oh, I don't know. They did celebrate when they found a safe haven. But I promise you a better dinner and a better dance floor than they'd have had."

He glanced up, realizing the crew had raised the flag and he hadn't even noticed. He took Tory's arm. "Let's see if I'm right."

"Lead on, Captain."

He stepped to the dock, then reached back to grasp her by the waist and swing her over. His hands fit neatly around her, and she clasped his arms for support.

"You didn't need to do that." She sounded slightly breathless. "I could have gotten out myself."

"Just trying to stay in character." He offered his arm. "Don't you think that's what your typical pirate would do?"

"Never having met one, I couldn't say." She slipped her hand into the crook of his arm. "I'll try and act the princess, but I'm not sure how gracefully I can manage this skirt."

"That was the first thing I thought when I saw you." The words came out without conscious consideration. "That night at the yacht club dance. You had on a white dress, and when you walked across the floor, you moved like a dancer."

She shook her head, and he thought she flushed a little. "You must have been dreaming."

"Maybe I was." They started up the steps. "But if so, it was a nice dream."

She glanced at him, her face very close to his as he opened the door. Her dark eyes were serious. "The trouble with dreams is that you have to wake up."

He pulled open one of the white double doors and

ushered her inside. "That doesn't mean you can't enjoy them."

Swashbuckler or not, that was what he intended to do. He'd leave all his native caution behind and, at least for tonight, enjoy the moment.

Jenny raced to them, cheeks flushed with excitement. "Aunt Sarah says can I sit with them for dinner? We're going to have sweet corn and watermelon and all the chicken we can eat. And afterward we're going to dance."

Matt and Sarah were probably matchmaking by taking Jenny off his hands, but at the moment he didn't care. "Okay, but you be good, you hear? And don't forget Miz Becky's going to take you home at eight o'clock."

Jenny pouted. "Can't I stay longer? I bet my cousins get to stay longer than that."

"I bet they don't." He ruffled her hair. "I know your Aunt Sarah and Uncle Matt too well to buy that. You run along now and have a good time."

She scampered off, and he turned to find Tory looking apprehensive. "You mean I have to eat sweet corn and watermelon in this dress? I wouldn't dare."

He couldn't help but laugh at her expression. "Sugar, it doesn't matter in the least if something gets spilled on that dress. But I expect they have more grown-up food, too. This is one time they try to satisfy everyone."

"If you say so." She looked doubtful.

"Take a look around." He gestured toward the crowd thronging through the double doors. The polished floor echoed to the sound of pirate boots, and the usually sedate yacht club echoed with laughter. "This party's for the whole island, and we're all set to celebrate together."

"A time when barriers come down," she said softly, and nodded toward the corner. "Do you see that?"

He followed the direction of her gaze, and his heart jolted with shock. His father and Uncle Clayton stood together. Alone together. Talking.

"I don't think I've ever seen that in my whole life," he said quietly, knowing his voice had roughened with telltale emotion. "None of us has."

"They look uncomfortable."

Tory sounded so anxious he squeezed her hand and then didn't want to let go. "I know they don't look like they did in that picture your mother drew. But just the fact that they're talking—" He stopped, knowing he could never make her understand how important this was. "Thank you, Tory. If you hadn't come, this might never have happened."

"You're the one who told your father to take that first step," she said. "It looks as if he listened to you."

"Yes, it does." He'd have said it was impossible, but it had happened. Maybe this was a time for miracles.

Tory pushed open the door to the ladies' room after dinner and paused, not sure whether to advance or retreat. It sounded as if someone was crying. A child. She moved quickly around the corner.

Jenny huddled in the corner of a wicker love seat, her shoulders shaking with sobs. Tory flew across the room.

"Jenny, what is it? Are you sick?"

Jenny's small face was blotchy from crying. "No," she muttered. "I want to go home!" A sob punctuated the word.

What had happened to the excited child who'd so looked forward to this evening? Tory's heart clenched. If someone had hurt Jenny...

She slid onto the couch and gathered Jenny against her. "Hush, now." She rocked her. "It'll be all right. Just tell me what happened."

Jenny sniffed, shaking her head.

"Come on, sugar," Tory coaxed, realizing she'd used Adam's pet name for his daughter. "You don't want me to bring your daddy in here, do you? He'd get in trouble for coming in the ladies' room."

That earned a watery giggle, and Jenny pulled back an inch so she could see Tory's face. "They were mean."

"Who was mean?" She stroked tangled curls from Jenny's face.

"We were dancing, me and Andi. We practiced and everything. We wanted to do a jig, like pirates do."

Tory nodded, remembering the girls dancing on the deck. "Well, that's a nice idea."

"It wasn't nice!" Jenny said, her lip trembling.

"There were some bigger boys watching us, and they made fun of us. They laughed at us!"

Something in Tory relaxed. Bruised pride was bad enough, but there were worse things. "Honey, you were right. They were mean."

"But I thought we danced right. I don't want people to laugh at me."

Tory drew her close. "I know, Jenny. People do that sometimes, and it hurts. Then you have to remember that what other people think doesn't matter all that much. It's what's in your heart that's important."

Jenny snuggled against her. "But I wanted to dance." Her voice was soft.

"And you will." Tory knew exactly what would make Jenny happy right now, because it was the same thing that would make her happy. "Come on, let's wash the tears away. Then you're going to dance with the handsomest man in the room."

A few minutes later they went, hand in hand, into the ballroom. Tory spotted Adam instantly. She seemed to have radar where he was concerned. She led Jenny to him.

"Captain, there's a young pirate here who really needs to dance with you." She put Jenny's hand in Adam's.

Adam sent one searching glance at his daughter's face and seemed to understand all the things Tory didn't say. In an instant he'd swept Jenny onto the floor.

Tory watched them, irresistibly reminded of that night so many years ago. She'd probably looked about as woebegone as Jenny did, coming into the dance all alone.

Now Jenny was smiling, eyes sparkling as she looked at her father. Adam twirled her around and around the floor. By the time the music ended they were both laughing.

Adam spun to a stop in front of Tory and caught Jenny in his arms for a kiss. "Thank you, Miz Jenny. That was the best dance of the night."

Jenny wiggled her way down. "I'm going to go tell Andi I was dancing. I think you should dance with Miz Tory now."

She darted off, and Adam held out his hand. "May I have this dance?"

It was what he'd said fifteen years before. And her heart seemed to be fluttering just as it had then.

No, she decided as she stepped into his arms. This Adam wasn't like the boy he'd been that night. He was a hundred times more exciting, and she was a hundred times more vulnerable.

"Thank you," he murmured, his breath stirring her hair. "Whatever it was, thank you."

"Jenny didn't tell you?"

He smiled. "I asked. She said I wouldn't understand. It was girl stuff. She said you made everything better."

"I suspect it was dancing with you that made her world all right."

He drew her closer into his arms. "Let's see if it has the same effect on you," he murmured, his lips brushing her cheek.

Her hand tightened on his shoulder as he swung her around. She felt strong muscle and warm skin through the fine fabric of his shirt. Warmth. Strength. Those words described Adam perfectly. He was a man a woman could depend on. Unfortunately, the woman who'd betrayed him still had those qualities entangled in the memory of that betrayal.

Tory wouldn't worry about that tonight. Adam's cheek was against hers, canceling out anything negative. She would follow her heart just this once.

Adam drew back an inch or two, enough to see her face. His gaze, mysterious as the ocean, lingered on each feature as if memorizing it, and her skin warmed.

"Remembering the last time we did this?" he asked softly.

"No." His lips were only a breath away from hers. "I'm just…enjoying the moment, that's all. Not thinking about the past. Just now."

His arm tightened around her. "That's what I've been telling myself all day. Seize the present. Don't worry about the past or the future."

"Can you do that?"

"I don't know." His eyes met hers honestly. "But I can try."

She tried not to let herself hope, but she couldn't seem to help it. "Maybe that's all any of us can do."

He didn't answer with words, but he drew her closer again. Their feet moved in perfect unison to the music, and she didn't know or care whether there was another person on the dance floor. Being here, with Adam, in this moment—that was enough.

The music stopped. She took a step back, disoriented, as if she'd wakened in a strange place from a very real dream.

Adam held her hand tightly. "Let's get a breath of air. This way."

The silk of her skirt whispered as they crossed the floor. Was anyone watching them, noting that Adam Caldwell was taking her onto the veranda? She didn't know, didn't care.

He swept her around him onto the dimly lit veranda, then closed the French doors. A patch of light, crosshatched by the small panes, fell onto wide boards. Still holding her hand, Adam led her toward the railing, where the only illumination was the pale moonlight.

He paused for an instant, picking up something from the wrought-iron table. Then he held it out to her—a white rose.

"I know we said we wouldn't think about the past." His voice was a touch rueful. "But somehow this seemed a fitting gesture."

Her heart was too full for words when she took the rose. She inhaled the sweet aroma and brushed velvety petals against her cheek. "That's a good memory." Her voice came out breathless. "I think we can hang on to that, can't we?"

He nodded. "You wore it in your hair. I'd try to put it there, but if I pricked you with a thorn, it might ruin the romantic gesture."

"I can manage." Her laugh was unsteady. She tucked the rose into the cluster of curls Miz Becky had pinned up what seemed an eon ago, knowing she wouldn't care if she did prick herself. "There."

"Beautiful." He touched the rose, then her cheek, his hand so gentle. "You're beautiful, Tory."

An automatic denial sprang to her lips. She wasn't beautiful, not like her mother. But she held the words back. Maybe it was time to give up that hurtful comparison for good.

Adam didn't seem to expect an answer. He cupped her chin in his hand, lifting it. He was going to kiss her.

A momentary panic swept her in a cold wave. She wasn't the Cinderella he remembered. And he wasn't ready, hadn't dealt with his feelings about his wife. They shouldn't.

Then his lips claimed hers, and her rational mind shut down entirely. Nothing remained but the moonlight, the faint strains of music and the strength of his arms around her. This wasn't about the past. This was about now.

Chapter Fourteen

This was just another part of the fairy tale, Tory told herself when she joined Adam's family at the public dock the next day after church. Being here, feeling a part of their clan, was a fantasy, not her ordinary life.

The warm Carolina sun beat down on her bare head, and she lifted a hand to shield her eyes. Philadelphia was probably cold and rainy, but here the weather insisted on apparently endless summer. It was all part of the fantasy.

The entire congregation of the Caldwell Cove church must have made its way to the dock. Some people carried flowers that fluttered in the breeze off the water. It should have been a festive scene, but people's expressions were serious, in contrast to yesterday's frivolity.

Jenny pressed close to her, slipping a small hand into hers. She smiled at the child, her heart warmed by the little sign of acceptance. She and Jenny seemed to have moved to a new place in their friendship since the incident at the yacht club.

"What happens next?" she whispered.

Jenny nodded to the water. "The boats will come. Watch for my daddy."

The crowd shifted a little, faces turning as if they'd received some sort of signal. Tory turned, the skirt of her dress fluttering in the breeze, and saw the first boat round the curve of the island and arrow toward the dock. Another followed it, then another, until the waterway was white with dozens of boats.

Jenny tugged at her hand and pointed. "See, there's Daddy," she whispered.

Adam was at the helm of the boat they'd taken the day they went to Angel Isle. He eased into the dock just below where they stood and cut his motor. Moving with that easy grace across the deck, he tossed a rope to the dock. His father caught it and made it fast.

Adam stood, his gaze seeming to search the crowd until he found them. He sketched a salute to Jenny. Then he gave Tory a small, private smile that made her heart tremble.

A fairy tale, she reminded herself desperately. It's just a fairy tale. But she was afraid her vulnerable heart wasn't listening.

One after another the boats moved in. She saw Adam's brother, then the Caldwell cousins, moor next to him. When every spot at the dock was taken, the boats formed a second row beyond the first, all of it accomplished with no sound but the creaking of timbers, the slap of the waves and the cries of the gulls.

When the last of the boats had been made fast, Pastor Wells stepped onto a makeshift platform at the end of the dock. As he lifted his hands to lead them in an opening prayer, Tory realized this really was a worship service. The blessing of the boats was an important part of the spiritual life of the island.

Everyone stood silent on the dock or in the boats as Pastor Wells began to read. A shiver made its way down Tory's spine. He was reading the names of all the islanders who'd died at sea.

She held Jenny's hand a little tighter. On the other side of the child, Adam's grandmother stood. Her face was strong, but tears filled her eyes as the names tolled on. With each name, those who carried flowers tossed them onto the water. The scent of the blossoms mingled with the salt air.

Her throat tight, Tory sought Adam's face again. He stood straight, almost at attention, his expression grave. This was a part of him she hadn't seen before—a part of island life she hadn't seen before. When he'd told her the family story about the shipwrecked sailor, she hadn't realized just what it meant. These people had lived, and died, by the sea for generations.

At last the reading of the names ended, and Pastor Wells lifted his hands again, facing the gathered boats. As he prayed for God's blessing on those who trod the sea, her heart seemed to overflow with her prayers and her almost incoherent longing to be a true part of this loving community.

Promptly after the amen, the choir began to sing the

hymn she'd heard more than once since she'd been on the island.

"Eternal Father, strong to save, whose arm has bound the restless wave…"

As the crowd joined in the hymn, those on the boats climbed onto the dock to join their families. Adam joined them, sweeping Jenny into his arms as he took his place between Tory and his grandmother. He reached down to clasp Tory's hand, holding it strongly as the hymn came to an end. The final amen floated over the water.

People started to move away, but Tory couldn't, not until she'd blinked away the last of the tears. Adam put Jenny down, said something quietly to his grand-mother, then turned to her.

"It's okay to cry, you know." He brushed a tear from her cheek. "I always do."

"I didn't realize what it was like." She swallowed hard, trying to get her voice to sound normal. "All those names."

He nodded, seeming to understand. "Even though I know it's coming, it still always hits me. How many we've lost over the years—some of them caught in storms, some through taking foolish chances. Some far away, like my grandfather's brother. He died on his ship at Pearl Harbor, but he's buried here."

She had trouble swallowing. "No wonder this place means so much to all of you."

"Gran says Caldwells are meant to come back to Caldwell Island no matter how far away they wander."

He looked at the waterway, and she followed his gaze. The flowers had floated into the center of the channel, carried by the tidal current. They formed a multicolored carpet on the green water.

"Did you ever think about going away?"

Adam shrugged. "I suppose every kid thinks once in a while of going out into the wide world to make his fortune. But I realized soon enough that all my dreams were here. My place, my family, my craft— everything I could want I found here on the island."

Still holding her hand, he began walking toward the street. Tory fell into step with him, wondering. Everything he could want, he'd said. Did he include his marriage in that list?

She couldn't ask. His bitterness toward Lila hadn't surfaced lately, and she hoped that meant he was coming to terms with it.

"What about you?" He looked at her with a question in his eyes.

"What about me what?"

"Your dreams," he prompted. "What are they, Tory?"

She could hardly say she thought her dreams were coming true when he kissed her the night before. It had been a kiss. No promises—just a kiss.

"Not very grand dreams, I suppose. Just the chance to do the work I love." She shrugged, thinking about it, and felt a wave of longing. "I guess I don't belong to a special place in the way you do with the island. My mother considered herself a Savannahian no matter where she lived. I like the city, but it's never felt like home to me.''

''Maybe you haven't found the right place yet.'' Their linked hands swung between them as they walked.

''Maybe,'' she agreed, but something in her heart cried. She'd found a place she wanted to call home. She'd found her soul mate.

She couldn't kid herself that she was pretending. She might not be Cinderella, but she'd found her Prince Charming.

Unfortunately, Adam didn't act as if he wanted anything deeper than a casual relationship. That would be fine, if not for the fact that she'd gone and fallen in love with him.

Adam couldn't deny the truth to himself. He was on his way home from the boatyard earlier than usual on Monday because he wanted to see Tory. Somehow she'd managed to flood his mind with memories of her face, her smile, her touch.

He didn't know where their relationship was going, and that was the honest truth. When Tory finished working on the window—

That was like running into a brick wall. When Tory finished the window, he'd have to face looking at it. And she was nearing that point. He'd heard her on the phone with Mona, talking about the progress she'd made.

He pulled through the gates of Twin Oaks and parked, then sat for a moment, staring through the windshield without really seeing. Okay, he could do this thing. It wouldn't be easy, but he'd find a way to cope with the memorial to Lila.

After all, he'd gotten through the years of sympathy, of people tiptoeing around his feelings because of the grief they assumed he bore. He'd get through this, too.

When Tory finished the window, she'd go away. The depth of his reaction to that startled him. He didn't want her to leave.

But he also wasn't prepared to ask her to stay. What that said about his emotional state he didn't want to consider.

He got out of the car and headed toward the house. He'd have to figure it out soon, or Cinderella would run out of his life again, just as she had before.

Jenny hurried to meet him on the porch, and he swung her up in his arms, planting a kiss of her soft cheek.

"How's my girl today?"

"I'm fine." She wiggled free and grabbed his hand, tugging at it. "Come on, Daddy. You have to come, right now."

He grinned, teasing her by hanging back. "Why do I have to come, sugar? What if I don't want to?"

She stamped her foot. "You have to, Daddy. Miz Tory wants us to come to the workroom."

He could feel the grin fade from his face. "Why does she?"

"The window!" Jenny practically bounced with excitement. "It's almost done, and she says we can see it. I wanted to go in already, but she said I had to wait until you got home. Now come!''

His stomach roiled. He'd known this moment was coming. He'd tried to fool himself that he was ready for it. He wasn't.

So much for his idea that he could live with this. He didn't want to see the window Tory had created for Lila, and he especially didn't want to see it with Jenny.

Resentment burned along his nerves as Jenny tugged him toward the stairway. Couldn't Tory have been a little more thoughtful? Didn't she realize how hard it would be to look at the window for the first time with Jenny?

Apparently she didn't. His jaw tightened until it felt ready to crack.

Tory stood outside the studio, waiting. She wore her usual jeans, this time with a cobalt-blue sweater. Her hands held each other tightly.

"Can I go in? Please, Miz Tory?"

Tory nodded, and Jenny darted into the room.

"Don't touch anything." He stopped next to Tory and lowered his voice. "Did you really have to set it up so that Jenny and I see this window at the same time?"

She whitened as if he'd hit her. "I think you've forgotten," she said evenly. "You were the one who told Jenny she'd be the first one to see it, as soon as it was ready."

The fact that he knew he was in the wrong didn't

make him feel any better. He ought to apologize. He couldn't.

"All right. Let's get this over with." He steeled himself for the inevitable.

Tory gave a curt nod. She turned and walked across the studio to the table, her back straight, her shoulders stiff.

He'd hurt her. He didn't know if he was angrier with her, with himself or with his mother-in-law for precipitating this.

Jenny stood on the opposite side of the table, hand hovering over the window as if she longed to touch it but knew she couldn't. "Look, Daddy," she breathed. "Just look."

He looked. The first thing he saw was the inscription at the base of the window.

In memory of Lila Marie Caldwell, beloved daughter, wife and mother.

Anger and betrayal burned in his heart like a physical pain. He'd thought he was over what Lila had done to him. He'd thought he was ready to try having a relationship with Tory.

How could he, when he was still filled with so much resentment?

"Oh, Daddy, look here. Isn't he beautiful?" Jenny clasped her hands together. "It's our dolphin."

He saw the joy on his daughter's face and finally looked at Tory's design. His breath caught.

The silver-gray dolphin soared from the waves, body curving in a perfect arc against the sky. The sensation of movement was so strong he could hardly convince himself the creature was made of glass. It was real, and yet somehow it was also the same dolphin carved by that first Caldwell so long ago.

"Yes," he said finally, choking out the word. "You're right, sugar. It is our dolphin." He managed to look at Tory, wanting to wipe the hurt from her eyes. "It's beautiful."

Relief swept across her face. Then Jenny hurtled into Tory's arms.

"I love it, Miz Tory. I just love it. Now everyone will be able to see the dolphin again."

Tory hugged her. "I'm glad you like it, sweetheart. I just have to finish the last few details, and then we'll be ready to put it up in the church."

"I'm going to tell Grandpa and Miz Becky about the window." Jenny danced to the door. "They'll be really happy, too."

Then she was gone, and he was alone with Tory and the memory of his harsh words. He had to apologize, had to tell her—

"Are you all right?" Her eyes, deep as brown velvet, assessed him.

For an instant his mind showed him how she'd looked in the moonlight when he kissed her. He had to force the image away so he could concentrate on the present.

"I think so." He swallowed, knowing he couldn't get through this easily. "I'm sorry. I did tell Jenny she could be the first to see it. I had no right to react the way I did."

She shook her head. "It's not a question of rights.

I know how hard it must be. I just—'' She spread her hands wide. ''You had to see it sometime.''

''You were right.''

''I was?'' She looked confused. ''About what?''

''When you first showed me the design. You said that it was as much for Jenny as for Lila. You said you thought it would honor the family.'' He nodded toward the dolphin. ''Jenny saw that as soon as she looked at the window. It just took me a little longer.''

Tory stared at him steadily, as if assessing whether or not he really meant his words. ''You said once that you couldn't walk into the church every Sunday and look at a memorial window for Lila. Has that changed?''

He tried to be honest with her, as well as with himself. ''I guess I'm not going to know exactly how I'll feel until it happens. The dedication will be hard.''

''People will expect you to talk about her.''

''Yes.'' That would be the hardest thing. ''But once it's over—'' He looked at her, trying to find the words that would tell her how he felt. ''Once it's over, I can forget about the dedication. I can concentrate on your beautiful dolphin, and just be thankful for it.''

The joy that flooded her eyes rewarded him. ''Thank you, Adam.'' Her voice was barely more than a whisper. ''I'm glad.''

He looked at the dolphin again, not letting his gaze stray toward the words. Tory should be able to feel pride in her work without being hampered by the emotions he couldn't seem to control.

''It really is beautiful, you know. I should think clients would be lining up with commissions for you.'' As soon as the words were out, it occurred to him that it sounded as if he wanted her to leave.

She glanced away. ''I'm afraid it's not so easy as that. People have to know the kind of work you can do. But it's a start. Now I have something all my own to show prospective clients.''

''Back in Philadelphia.''

She looked at him, startled. ''Of course.''

He shouldn't say anything. He didn't know where they were going or whether anything could come of this. But he couldn't let her walk away again.

''Do you have to go back? Couldn't you work somewhere else? Like here?''

Tory's heart seemed to stop beating as Adam's words penetrated. He wanted her to stay.

Careful, she thought, careful. Don't jump to conclusions that could hurt and embarrass both of you. Find out what's on his mind.

''I...I don't know what you mean.'' She hated the fact that she sounded so hesitant. What had happened to her prized independence?

Adam looked as if he were struggling with what he meant, too. Before he could speak, quick footsteps sounded in the hallway.

''Adam, dear! Ms. Marlowe! I just couldn't stay away any longer. Once Tory told me it was nearly finished, I had to see the memorial for myself.'' Adam's mother-in-law fluttered into the room and threw her arms around him.

Mixed emotions flooded through Tory. Of course her client had every right to see the window she'd commissioned. The natural apprehension as to whether the woman would be pleased with her work mingled with a dread of what this might do to Adam's precarious acceptance of the memorial. Was he going to be able to handle this?

"Mona, I didn't expect…" Adam seemed to censor his words. "It's good to see you. If you'd let me know you were coming, I'd have met you at the airport."

Mrs. Telforth took a step back, patting his cheek. "My dear, I didn't want to trouble you."

She spun to Tory, holding out both hands. "Tory, dear." She looked as she had each time Tory had seen her—elegant and expensive from the top of her carefully tinted ash-blond hair to the tips of her handmade Italian shoes.

"Mrs. Telforth, how are you?" *Why didn't you warn us you were coming? And will your presence complicate an already difficult situation?*

"Fine, fine." She glanced around the room. "Is it finished? Can I see?"

Adam's smile was so stiff it looked as if it would break. "It's almost finished. I think you'll be pleased with what Tory's accomplished." He took her arm and led her toward the table.

Tory followed, an incoherent prayer forming in her heart. *Please, please.*

Adam and his mother-in-law stopped at the edge of the table. For a long moment no one said anything.

Then Mrs. Telforth clasped both hands together in a gesture that reminded Tory of Jenny.

"It's beautiful. Oh, Adam, isn't it just beautiful? Wouldn't Lila have loved it?"

From where she stood, Tory could see the muscle twitching in his jaw. "Yes," he said evenly. "I'm sure she'd have been pleased."

Mrs. Telforth blotted tears with a lace handkerchief. "I wanted so much to have a memorial to her here, on the island, where her life was. Read the inscription for me, dear."

His pain reached across the distance between them to grasp Tory's throat as she read aloud.

His gaze met Tory's over his mother-in-law's bowed head, and whatever hope had lingered in her heart turned to dust. All the light had gone out of him. He looked as stern and unforgiving as the sea.

Chapter Fifteen

Tory crossed the workroom hours later to stare out the window at the darkening sky. Streaks of pink and purple, painted across the horizon, bathed the island in the gathering dusk. Soon it would be full dark.

Soon it would be time for her to leave. Her throat tightened. The window was finished. Once it was installed in the church, there was no reason for her to be here.

A few hours ago she'd stood in this room and heard Adam ask her to stay. She shook her head. That had been real, hadn't it?

She pressed her hand against her heart. Adam had shut down at the sight of his mother-in-law. She didn't think he was going to open up again. Whatever he'd intended to say to her had been wiped out.

"Tory."

At the sound of his voice, her treacherous heart persisted in filling with unreasonable hope. She turned to find him crossing the workroom toward her.

"Why did you disappear from dinner so quickly?"

Because it hurt too much to see you. "Well, I...I thought it was a time for family."

A shadow crossed his face as he stood next to her at the window. "Mona's arrival was a surprise."

Not a welcome one, to judge by his expression. "You said once she acted on whim."

He shrugged, managing a smile. "That's Mona. Still, it's good for Jenny to spend a little time with her, I guess."

"Of course." Jenny had been obviously entranced with the arrival of her grandmother, and she'd spent the entire dinner hour filling her in on everything she'd done in the last month.

"She won't stay long," he said. "She never does."

The last thing she wanted to do was have a casual conversation with Adam about his late wife's mother. Or anything else, for that matter. She wanted to know what he'd been going to say before Mona had come fluttering into the studio. She couldn't ask.

Adam shook his head, as if to chase away his thoughts. "We never got to finish our conversation this afternoon. About you not leaving."

"I don't..." She stopped, collected her thoughts. Adam would have to be clearer than that. "My job is almost finished. Why would I stay?"

He looked uncomfortable at the direct question. "You've been working hard. Don't you deserve a little vacation?"

She tried not to let disappointment show on her face. Adam was being kind. Everyone knew he was always kind.

"Whether I deserve it or not, I don't think I can afford it. I've got a struggling business to get on its feet, remember?"

Struggling was certainly the word. The amount she'd receive from this job would about cover the final expenses she owed from her mother's illness and death without much left over to pay the rent. "I have to start looking for my next commission."

"Is there any reason you can't do that from here? As far as I can see, your business is pretty much in your own hands."

She turned toward the window. It had gotten darker in the last few minutes, and she hoped the darkness hid her face. Adam was more right about that than he probably knew. Marlowe Stained Glass Studio consisted of her business cards, her small cache of equipment and her own two hands. She could work from anywhere.

But there was a very good reason that anywhere shouldn't be here. She'd done the last thing she should have done—she'd fallen in love with a man who wasn't ready to love again.

She couldn't let him guess that. Unfortunately, she'd never been especially good at hiding what she felt.

"I guess it's true that I can take my work anywhere." She wasn't any good at beating around the bush, either. She swung to face him. "Why would you ask me to stay? Given the reason I came, I should think you'd be glad to see the last of me.''

His expression softened, his lips slipping into a rueful smile. ''Come on, Tory. You know that's not true. With you around, I'm starting to feel seventeen again. You can't tell me you're not feeling that way, too.''

''I guess not, but...'' She'd begun to hope until Mona Telforth had fluttered into the workroom. ''I had the sense Mona's arrival changed things.''

Adam's jaw tightened. ''I can't deny seeing her threw me. But after the initial shock passed, I realized it didn't have to change anything. Mona is Jenny's grandmother, so she'll always be part of our lives, but the past is past. Maybe it's time to move beyond it.''

Could he? Or was he fooling himself? And her.

Adam's step covered the space between them, and he took both of her hands in his. ''We can't go back to our past, either. But I'd like for us to have a chance to get to know each other again.''

The fluttering began in the pit of her stomach and spread to her heart. How could she answer that?

Unfortunately she was way ahead of him. She didn't need time to get to know Adam again. She felt as if she'd already known him forever—known him and loved him. If he didn't feel the same, was any amount of time going to change that?

''Please.'' His voice deepened, and the tone set her nerves vibrating in response. ''That's what happened before. You left, and we never had a chance to find out what might happen between us. I don't want it to be that way again.''

She took a breath, trying to think beyond the clamor of her emotions. Trying to stifle the voice that said she should grab this opportunity and hold fast because it wouldn't come again.

"I guess." She steadied her voice. "I guess I can stay until the new window is dedicated, at least."

And after that?

She'd probably find herself leaving Caldwell Island with a broken heart. But that was a sure thing anyway, wasn't it?

"Okay, I think that's going to do it." Tory stepped back from the frame for the new window, nodding to the carpenter who'd spent the morning working in the church with her. "I'll see you tomorrow to install it."

As the man gathered his tools, she heard a quick step behind her. She turned to find Miranda Caldwell crossing the sanctuary toward her.

"Hey, Tory." Miranda gazed at the empty frame. "Is the new window really ready to go up?"

"Just about." Tory's nerves jumped to attention. Did Miranda wonder why she was still here, in that case? What would the rest of the Caldwell clan think about her staying on at Twin Oaks? They might already be speculating about it. "We'll put it in tomorrow. That's always the scary part, when you visualize hours of work shattering. Pray that it goes well."

"I will. I have been." Miranda's green eyes, so like her cousin's, focused on Tory's face. "I hear you're staying around for a while."

The island grapevine must work very efficiently. "I thought I'd stay until the dedication, anyway."

Miranda clasped her hand warmly. "I'm glad, Tory. You're good for him, you know."

She couldn't pretend not to know what Miranda was talking about. "I hope so."

"I know so. Believe me, I know my cousin."

Tory glanced upward, her gaze focusing on the image of Jesus walking on the water. Unconditional love shone in His face as He reached toward Peter.

Is that what I've come here to find, Lord? That kind of love?

"Maybe," she said aloud.

"Trust," Miranda said softly. "Just trust."

Tory blinked back sudden tears. She and Miranda seemed able to speak to each other from the heart, and that was a precious thing. "I'm trying."

Miranda nodded. "Okay, then. Oh, I almost forgot why I'm here, besides my abundant curiosity." She thrust an envelope toward Tory. "This came to the inn for you. I thought it might be important."

"Thank you." She took the envelope, frowning at the return address. Why was *Glass Today* magazine writing to her?

Miranda gave her a quick hug. "Don't forget. Trust." She was gone before Tory could respond.

Trust. She looked at the window again. *I'm trying, Lord.*

She ripped open the envelope, pulled out the single sheet of paper and stared at it in disbelief. *Glass Today* magazine wanted to do a story about her work in the

Caldwell Cove church. She'd mentioned the project when she'd run into the magazine's photographer at a glass show. He'd seemed interested, but she never expected this.

She blinked back the tears that threatened to spill over. This was an opportunity she hadn't had the nerve to dream of. If her work was featured in the magazine, she'd find the church commissions she longed for. She'd be able to create her own songs of praise in the windows she made, like the craftsmen who'd done the windows in this church so long ago.

Thank you. Thank you.

She looked around, feeling as if the news would explode from her if she didn't share it with someone. And then she realized she did have someone to share it with. She could tell Adam. Even if he wasn't ready yet to claim more than friendship between them, he'd be happy for her. They would celebrate together.

Did he have any idea what he was doing where Tory was concerned? Adam leaned against the workbench, absently running his hand along the planking for the new boat. The converted warehouse he used for construction was silent. Most of the crew had gone home already, making this a good time and place to think.

Except that thinking didn't seem to be getting him very far. Every time he tried to assess his relationship with Tory, his errant imagination presented him with an image of her face, tipped up to his in the moonlight. Her dark eyes seemed to promise love, comfort, understanding, faithfulness—all the things he'd believed he had once.

He seized the plane, feeling muscles flex as he ran it along the plank, the fresh smell of sawdust mingling with the salt air. He'd better concentrate on work, since he couldn't think about Tory without getting emotions tangled up in it.

Who was he kidding? Everything about Tory had to do with emotions. He'd asked her to stay, but he could hardly expect her to hang around here while he tried to decide if they had a future. She had a right to more than that.

He wanted to believe he could love again. But he'd run on autopilot for the last four years, telling himself he had enough in life with his family, his business and his responsibilities. He stopped planing, letting his palm rest on the warm wood. Since Tory came, he'd realized that wasn't enough. What he didn't know was whether he was ready for more.

Why not, some part of his mind demanded. Why can't you move on? Why can't you move on with Tory?

Tory wasn't Lila. She wasn't anything like Lila. Tory understood.

He heard the creak of the wooden door, and something told him it was Tory before he turned around. She stood in the doorway for a moment, the light behind her, and he couldn't make out her face.

Then she moved quickly toward him, and he read the joy in her expression.

"Hey." He rested a hip against the workbench, enjoying the sight of her. "It's good to see you."

"You almost didn't. The boatyard looks deserted. I thought you'd gone home, but then I spotted your truck."

"I wanted to get in an hour on the hull of the new boat." He patted the smooth wood. "If I do it when people are here, they keep interrupting me."

"Like me?" She lifted those level brows.

"You're a welcome interruption." He reached for her, taking her hand and drawing her closer to lean against the workbench next to him. "I'm always glad to see you."

Funny, that she'd become such an important part of his life in such a short period of time. They'd had a head start, though. Maybe subconsciously he'd always remembered his Cinderella.

"That's good." She let her hand rest companionably in his, apparently content to enjoy the moment.

That was one of the things that drew him to her—that certain stillness. Maybe it was the artist in her, letting her look with appreciation at dust motes floating in a shaft of sunshine from the high windows.

"This is a nice place," she said finally. "It feels like good work is done here."

"I hope so." He shifted so he could look more fully in her face. Those strong bones of cheek and jaw would give her a distinctive beauty even when she was as old as Gran. And how far gone was he that he even thought such a thing? He brushed a lock of dark brown hair from her cheek. "Of course it's not quite as nice as working in the church, now, is it?"

She turned to look at him, her soft cheek moving against his fingers. "That reminds me why I came. I got some exciting news. I wanted to share it with you."

Something vaguely uneasy touched him, like a cold chill on the back of his neck. "News about what?"

She pulled an envelope from the pocket of her denim jacket. "This came to the inn for me, and Miranda brought it over. It's from *Glass Today* magazine."

"The magazine that did that spread on your old boss?" He remembered as he said it that the man had also been her old fiancé. He hadn't deserved a woman like Tory.

She nodded, and happiness danced in her eyes as she filled him in on her good news. "I know one of their photographers, and I guess she suggested a story. It just came out of the blue."

The chill intensified. "A story? What kind of a story?"

If warning sounded in his voice, she obviously didn't hear it. She gestured, her hands opening an imaginary magazine. "A photo layout of the church, with pictures of the restored windows and a bit of information about the original artist, if they can find it. But mostly it will be about the new window—interviews, photos, everything."

"Interviews," he repeated. His stomach roiled. Interviews about Lila, probably.

She must have heard his tone. Caution dampened the excitement in her face.

"That's what they usually do." She eyed him as if trying to read his mind.

He pressed both hands hard against the wooden bench behind him. "Tory, you can't let them do that."

She blinked, looking at him without understanding. "What do you mean?"

"Just what I said." He used his hands to launch his body away from the bench, unable to stand still a moment longer. "No article, Tory."

"You can't be serious." She flung her hands out. "Don't you understand what this means to me? This will open the door to all sorts of church jobs for me. I can do what I've always dreamed of doing."

"You're the one who doesn't understand. They'll want to write about Lila. They'll want to interview us. Can you imagine what Mona would say? They'd probably even want a picture of Jenny. You can't let them do that. *I* can't!"

"But you agreed to the window. You said you could handle this."

His jaw clenched so tightly it was painful. "I guess I was wrong, then. Maybe I can cope with seeing that window in the church, but I can't cope with this. I won't have my family put on display in a magazine for all the world to see."

"It's not…"

"Tory—" He stopped, took a breath, tried to think through the maze of emotions that tumbled inside him. "Tory, I love you. If you love me, you'll give this up."

Chapter Sixteen

Adam's words echoed like a death knell. He loved her, but— The pain deepened, like a sliver of glass driving into Tory's heart. He would only love her if she did what he wanted, like her grandmother, like her mother, like Jason.

She looked at him. His usually laughing eyes were as hard as flint.

She could have what she wanted. She could have his love. All she had to do was accept the conditions that came with it. A longing swept over her to do just that.

"No." She didn't realize she was going to say it aloud until she heard the word echo in the still, cavernous space. It ricocheted from the high ceiling and clanged against the walls.

Adam looked taken aback. "No what?"

"No." She knew what she had to say, and her heart

shattered with the knowledge. "It's not love if it comes with strings attached."

If that hurt him, he didn't show it. No feeling stirred in his usually expressive face. "You're going to go ahead with this, knowing how I feel."

She had to fight the wave of exhaustion that swept over her. Even shaking her head took an effort. She didn't want to fight any more. She wanted—oh, how she wanted—to pretend she could believe he truly loved her. But she couldn't. Real love wasn't preceded by the word *if*.

"I'll turn down the article."

He took a quick step toward her, his face lightening. "Tory, I'll make it up to you."

She stopped him with an outflung hand. "No." She pushed the word out, swimming against the tide of longing to be in his arms. "I'll give up the article not because I think it's right, but because it matters so much to you. But I don't want anything else from you."

He went still. "I don't understand."

She wouldn't let herself cry, not in front of him. She forced her voice to be steady. "I don't want love that comes with conditions, Adam. If I've learned anything, I've learned that."

"I'm just asking you not to do something that will hurt my family."

"We both know that's not what this is about." She breathed a prayer. *Please, Lord. Let me say what needs to be said.*

Anger sparked in his eyes. "You'd better tell me, because I don't know what you mean."

Somehow Adam's anger stiffened her spine. "This isn't about family. It's about your bitterness toward Lila."

"All right, I can't forgive her." He almost shouted the words, then seemed to realize what he'd done and clamped his mouth closed. "I can't forgive her," he repeated quietly. "How could I?"

"I don't know. I haven't done so well in the forgiveness department myself." She closed her eyes for an instant, gathering strength. "But I know you can't love anyone else as long as you can't forgive Lila."

Adam's face tightened until it resembled a wooden mask, stiff and impenetrable. "Then I guess I'm not going to love anyone."

She wanted to cry out to him, wanted to tell him not to throw away what they might have together. But she couldn't. This was a battle he'd have to fight alone.

Help him, Lord, because I can't.

"Goodbye, Adam." She turned and moved blindly toward the door, feeling the hot tears spill onto her cheeks and knowing she'd lost him.

Adam accelerated until he could hear nothing but the roar of the boat's motor, feel nothing but the rush of wind against his body. He rounded the curve of the island and headed toward open water.

It didn't work. No noise was loud enough to drown out Tory's voice. He'd been trying to do that for nearly twenty-four hours, and he couldn't. If he ran the boat all the way to the Florida Keys, he wouldn't outrun Tory's words.

He eased back on the throttle, slowing until the boat bounced gently on the incoming tide, then cut the motor and let the boat drift. The endless, inexorable waves rolled toward him, gray and green as the waves in the church window of Jesus walking on the water. He'd looked at that image a thousand times without really seeing it until Tory, with her artist's eyes, had made him see.

Peter, drowning in his lack of faith. Something cold clutched Adam's heart. He looked at the waves and imagined what it would be like.

No, he didn't have to imagine. He knew. He'd been out of the boat himself—once in a fishing accident, once in a storm. He'd felt the current grab him, known his clothes were dragging him down, struggled in panic against the tide. He'd been in the place of all those islanders who'd been lost at sea.

But he hadn't drowned. Each time someone had been there to help him. Like Peter, he hadn't drowned.

Until now.

Peter had been sinking under the weight of his lack of faith. Adam was sinking under the weight of his lack of forgiveness.

Everything in him rose to reject that thought. He couldn't forgive. Anger and bitterness clutched his heart. What Lila had done to him was unforgivable.

Unforgivable? He saw, in his mind's eye, the face of Jesus in the window. Jesus looked at Peter without regard for Peter's failings—He looked at Peter with unconditional love.

Tory didn't deserve love that came with conditions. She was wise enough to know that wasn't love at all.

He had to free himself. But he couldn't. He stared at the rolling waves, tears salty as the ocean filling his eyes.

Please, Lord. I can't do it myself. Please, help me learn to forgive. Help me.

"Easy, easy." Tory held her breath as the workmen put the new window into its frame. It creaked as if in protest, and then settled into place.

She couldn't look at it. Her beautiful dolphin only gave her pain instead of joy.

She took a step back, letting the workmen secure the window. She wouldn't have to see it much longer. Her bags were packed. As soon as this was finished, she'd leave Caldwell Island. This time she wouldn't be back.

I failed. The thought haunted her. She hadn't found the dolphin, hadn't kept her promise to her mother.

She'd finished the commission, but at a cost she'd be feeling for the rest of her days.

She covered her eyes with her palms only to see the colored light from the windows against the darkness.

She dropped her hands and stared at the image of Jesus walking on the water. His loving gaze, directed at Peter, seemed to touch her, too. It was as if He spoke directly to her wounded heart.

You have unconditional love from Me, dear child. Forgive yourself, and be content.

Love flowed through her, easing the pain. She could see more clearly.

She couldn't erase the pain of her mother's life, no matter how much she longed to. She couldn't undo Emily's past. But she couldn't regret her time here, no matter how much it hurt. She'd done the right thing in coming back to Caldwell Island.

Tory looked at her dolphin, springing from the waves. She hadn't found the lost carving, but she'd done what she could. It had to be enough.

"I see it's finished."

At the sound of Adam's voice, her hands clenched, fingernails biting into the palms. How long would it be until she could think of him without pain?

She turned to watch as he came slowly down the center aisle. Through the pain, she stored up one more image of him to carry away with her. It would have to last a long time.

She was vaguely aware of the workmen gathering their tools. The moment they took to exchange a few words with Adam gave her time to armor herself. The door closed behind the workmen, and they were alone in the church. They'd come full circle.

"Yes. It's done." There didn't seem to be anything else to say. She'd already said it all. "I'll be leaving today."

"I don't think you should go so soon." Adam took a step closer. "The photographer won't be here until tomorrow."

It was hard to think with him so close. "Photographer?"

"From the magazine. I called them. They're going to do the story."

She looked at him, not quite able to believe what she was hearing. "You called them? But why? I told you I'd give up the story."

"You told me it wasn't love if it came with strings attached."

Her words came back to hurt her, and she swallowed hard. "I told you I'd give it up," she said again. "You didn't have to call them."

"Yes, I did."

She didn't dare to hope. "Why?"

His strong face grew bleak. "I wanted to take the easy way out. I thought I could accept the memorial and pretend that my life with Lila was behind me. That I could just forget."

His words pierced her heart. "Forgetting doesn't work, does it?" The Lord knew she'd tried that.

"No." He clenched his jaw. "I couldn't forget. You were right. I had to forgive first."

"I'm glad," she said carefully, not able to let herself hope. "If you're able to forgive Lila, I'm glad." The emotions roiling through her were too big, too scary.

"I had to forgive so I could free my heart to love again." He lifted his hand to touch her cheek gently. "It's the only way I could offer you my love. Unconditionally."

She searched his face, longing to believe and not

quite daring to. But the steady light in his eyes told her the truth. He meant what he said. He loved her.

With a little sob, she stepped into his arms. "You mean it."

He held her close, his cheek against hers. "I love you, Tory Marlowe. Please say you can love me."

She'd come to Caldwell Cove to find the secrets of the past. God had shown her the secrets of the heart.

She looked at Adam, heart almost too full to speak. "I can," she managed to say. "I do."

Epilogue

A few weeks ago, Adam wouldn't have dreamed he'd be able to do this. He stood near the pulpit in the church, waiting his turn to speak at the dedication of the new window.

He hadn't thought he could even look at the window, but now his heart was drawn toward Tory's beautiful creation. The dolphin rose from the sea, even more dramatic seen as it should be, with the sunlight behind it and the colors streaming across the faces of the people he loved.

His brother, his cousins, their spouses and children—every Caldwell had come. His heart swelled as he looked at his father sitting next to Uncle Clayton. They'd taken another faltering step in finding a relationship, sitting together in church for the first time since they were boys. The joy in Gran's face was almost too intense to behold.

Music from the organ filled the sanctuary until it

seemed the walls must breathe with it. Soon the organist would finish, and it would be his turn to speak. He'd have to talk about Lila.

He could, now. Loving Tory had let him find his way to forgiveness and peace.

Tory sat in the front row, between Mona and his daughter. The engagement ring he'd given her sparkled in the light from the window, and it occurred to him how appropriate that was. The window had brought Tory back to him.

They'd settled so many things in the last few weeks. Tory would continue to create her stained glass in the larger studio he was building where she could have both a workroom and a display area. She'd travel when she had to, but most of the time she'd be on the island, where she belonged.

His heart filled with thankfulness as he looked at her serene profile. God had given them such a precious gift in their love for each other.

Tory turned her head, her gaze seeking his, and gave him a small, private smile. For an instant some trick of the light turned her into the young girl in the white dress with stars in her eyes.

His Cinderella. He'd found her and lost her fifteen years ago, but when the time was right, God had brought her home to him at last.

* * * * *

Be sure to watch for Miranda's story,
coming only to Love Inspired
in May 2003.

And now for a sneak preview,
please turn the page.

Chapter One

Tyler Winchester ripped open the pale blue envelope that had arrived in the morning mail. A photograph fluttered onto the polished mahogany desktop. No letter, just a photograph of a young boy, standing in the shade of a sprawling live oak.

He flipped it over. Two words had been scrawled on the back—two words that made his world shudder.

Your son.

For a moment he couldn't react at all. He shot a glance toward the office doorway, where his younger brother was trying to talk his way past Tyler's assistant. Turning his back on them, Tyler studied the envelope. Caldwell Cove. The envelope was postmarked Caldwell Cove, South Carolina.

Something deep inside him began to crack painfully open. The child's face in the picture was partly shadowed by the tree, but that didn't really matter. He saw the resemblance anyway—the heart-shaped face, the pointed chin. Miranda.

The boy was Miranda's child, certainly. But his? How could that be? He'd have known. She'd have told him, wouldn't she?

The voices behind him faded into the dull murmur of ocean waves. A seabird called, and a slim figure came toward him from the water, green eyes laughing, bronze hair rippling over her shoulders.

His jaw clenched. No. He'd closed off that emotional corner of himself a long time ago, sealing it securely. He wouldn't let it break open.

The truth was, he didn't know what Miranda might do. It had been—what, eight years? He stared at the photo. The boy could be the right age.

He spun around, his movement startling both his brother and his assistant into silence. Josh took advantage of the moment to move past Henry Carmichael's bulk. He looked from Tyler's face to the photo in his hand, gaze curious. "Is something wrong?"

"Nothing." Nothing that he wanted to confide in Josh, in any event. He slid the photograph into his pocket.

"In that case…"

"Not now." He suspected he already knew what Josh wanted to talk about. Money. It was always money with Josh, just as it was with their mother and with the array of step and half siblings and relatives she'd brought into his life. The whole family saw Tyler as an inexhaustible account to fund their expensive tastes.

You can't count on anyone but yourself. His father's harsh voice echoed in his mind. They all want something.

"But Tyler..." Josh began.

He shook his head, then looked at Henry. He could at least trust Henry to do what he was told without asking questions that Tyler had no intention of answering. "Have the jet ready for me in two hours. I'm flying to Savannah."

"Savannah?" Josh's voice suggested it might as well be the moon. "What about the Warren situation? I thought you were too involved in that contract negotiation to think about anything else."

He spared a thought for the multimillion-dollar deal he'd been chasing for months. "I'll be a phone call or fax away. Henry will keep me posted on anything I need to know."

"Whatever you say." Henry's broad face was impassive as always. Henry was as unemotional as Tyler, which was probably why they worked so well together.

Tyler crossed the room quickly, pausing to pull his camel-hair coat from the mahogany coatrack. It had been a raw, chilly March day in Baltimore, although Caldwell Cove would be something else.

Again the image shimmered in his mind like a mirage. Surf. Sand. A laughing, sun-kissed face. His wife.

They all want something. What did Miranda want?

He shoved the thought away and strode to the door. He'd deal with this, just as he dealt with any project that went wrong. Then he'd bury the memory of his first love so deeply that it would never intrude again.

Dear Reader,

Thank you for choosing to pick up this book. I hope you've enjoyed the story of Adam and Tory. I've had such pleasure in writing the Caldwell clan stories that I'll hate to leave them when the stories are finished.

I began thinking about this story when I took a class in making stained glass a few years ago. Although I'll never be the artist that Tory is, learning about the glass has given me a new appreciation for the wonderful works that grace so many sanctuaries.

I love to hear from readers, and I'd be happy to send you a signed bookplate and let you know when my books are coming out. You can reach me c/o Steeple Hill Books, 300 East 42nd St., 6th Floor, New York, NY 10017 or visit me on the Web at www.martaperry.com.

Blessings,

Marta Perry

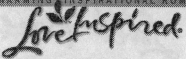